We came all the way from Cuba
so you could dress like this?

We came all the way from Cuba so you could dress like this?

STORIES BY

Achy Obejas

CLEIS
PRESS

Published in the United States by Cleis Press Inc., P.O. Box 8933, Pittsburgh, Pennsylvania 15221, and P.O. Box 14684, San Francisco, California 94114.

Book design and production: Pete Ivey
Cover illustration: Nereyda Garcia-Ferraz
Cleis logo art: Juana Alicia

First Edition.
Printed in the United States.
10 9 8 7 6 5 4 3 2 1

"Wrecks" appears in *Girlfriend Number One* (Cleis Press), edited by Robin Stevens.
"Above All, A Family Man" appears, in slightly different form, in *ACM* 26 (Fall 1993).
"Man Oh Man" was adapted for the stage in 1990 by Zebra Crossing Theater, Chicago.
"The Spouse" appears, in slightly different form, in *Discontents* (Amethyst), edited by Dennis Cooper.
"We Came All the Way from Cuba So You Could Dress Like This?" appears in *Michigan Quarterly Review*/Puentes a Cuba, Vol. II (September 1994).

Library of Congress Cataloging-in-Publication Data
Obejas, Achy, 1956–
    We came all the way from Cuba so you could dress like this? / by Achy Obejas.
        p. cm.
    ISBN 0-939416-92-1 : $24.95.
    —ISBN 0-939416-93-X (pbk.) : $10.95
    1. Cuban American women—Fiction. 2. Lesbians—United States—Fiction.
PS3565.P34W4 1994
813'.54—dc20   94-18194
                                                              CIP

For Diane, who made all the difference.

Contents

Acknowledgements

Thanks to Felice Newman, Frédérique Delacoste, and everyone at Cleis; Charlotte Sheedy; and Doug Sadownik (for making all the right introductions).

Thanks, too, to Robert Boswell, Joan Silber, Michael Martone, Chuck Wachtel, Connie Porter, Karen Brennan, Jim Shepard, Charles Baxter, Mary Elsie Robertson, and everyone at Warren Wilson College.

I am also grateful to the National Endowment for the Arts, Illinois Arts Council, Corporation of Yaddo, the Ragdale Foundation, Jeffrey McCourt, Marianna Murphy Kohl, *Chicago Reader*, *Chicago Tribune*, and Columbia College.

Finally, I want to thank Melvin Plotinsky, Nena Torres, Nereyda Garcia-Ferraz, Gini Sorrentini, Susanna Ruth Berger and Tom Asch, Jorge Casuso, Maria Kostas, Donna Blue Lachman, Susan Nussbaum, my cousin Adriana Busot, my brother Mario, and Cathy Edelman, my own little Rock of Gibraltar.

Wrecks

I have to be sure I have the right insurance—that is, collision as well as liability. I simply can't afford not to be able to pay for whatever car repairs I might need, and I'm afraid that sooner or later (and probably sooner) I'm going to be sitting in a mechanic's waiting room, right there next to the Coke machine and the faded road maps, flipping through some weathered copy of *Time* or *Popular Mechanics*, waiting to be told what my insurance will and won't cover.

This is very important to me right now because I always have an automobile accident after a break-up, and Sandra, my lover of five years, just left me for some babe who lives in San Francisco, the promised land of fruit and nuts. We were one of those couples everyone envied—good-looking, funny, successful—so I'm still trying to figure out how this happened, and why. Sandra's dark, jealous, and bird-like, as impatient and breathtaking as a nestling, and the new babe is tall and wooden. I know I shouldn't dwell on it—it's not good for me—but I *know* they don't fit.

Since Sandra moved out on me in order to pump up her phone bill and become a free and frequent flyer, I've been trying to take the bus and train everywhere—to work, to the post office, even to the grocery store, which I hate doing because, since I can't carry ten bags of stuff with the same ease with which I can pack them into the VW, I end up having to do some shopping every time I leave the house. Since I'm trying to be environmentally conscious and use paper bags, which don't have handles, this is doubly tough on the five block walk from the store to my apartment.

The last time this happened was about seven years ago. It had been three and a half years of utter hell with Loretta, but I still couldn't believe she'd really left, so in my grief and disbelief I wrapped my car around a tree in a south Chicago suburb. I did it the minute Loretta left for Los Angeles, a city in which no one is actually born but to which millions are drawn like moths to a fire. Loretta was lithe, a singer with an immense and angry voice. I'd always thought we shared a cosmic connection of some sort: after all, we fought and fucked like minks. But she said she had to go because she'd imagined women would be kinder than men, and my sarcasm was wearing on her sense of sisterhood.

To make matters worse, after I'd wrapped my car around the tree, I refused to believe it was inoperable, so I did my damndest to start it, sending the fan blades tearing through the radiator, which had been pushed up a good six inches. The entire mess cost me around two thousand dollars, including the towing fee back to the city. I should have just chucked the car—a beat up mustard-colored Dodge Valiant—but I didn't. I just kept going. So did Loretta, who married the corporate lawyer for Hughes Aircraft. They have two daughters now, one inexplicably named after me. I confess it does give me comfort: it's evidence of sorts that I had an effect on that girl after all.

Before that, when Doris left me for membership in a lesbian separatist living collective somewhere in the hills of Arkansas, I made a point of not seeing the steel post holding up the chain around one of Chicago's lakefront parks. I knew Doris and I had problems living together—she smoked with the same fatal simmer of an arsoned building, leaving powdery ash sculptures everywhere—but it seemed extreme that my nagging should drive her to repentance in a place where no cigarettes, polyester, or dairy products are allowed.

After Doris left, I'd wanted just to drive leisurely and miserably through the park, which was—wisely, I suppose—closed for the winter. I just wanted to get a look at the lake, frozen with the waves mid-roll. I knew they'd remind me of all those little ash tubes, gray and mindless, that Doris had left around the house. But I never made it to the lakefront. I ended up sliding on some ice on the road and sort of hopping onto one of the little posts that held up the keep-out chain, ramming the post through the transmission of my car and causing total vehicular loss. Ultimately, I didn't mind so much. I hadn't yet noticed car accidents as a post-relationship pattern, and I'd never much liked that car anyway, a green and white Gremlin that looked like a pimp shoe.

To be honest, I think the whole accident/relationship thing really started after a brief affair with a former sports writer for the *Chicago Sun-Times* whom everybody thinks is bisexual but who is really a lesbian. She'd cover Bulls games by watching them in her peripheral vision on TV while lying on top of me on her bed. After she moved to Washington, D.C., to cover society happenings, I ran my old Chevy van into the line of taxis waiting across the street from the *Sun-Times* building, giving the domino theory a whole new twist.

I don't drive anything as lethal as a van now, but rather my more benign, if not just plain cartoonish, VW bug, one of the original Beetles, red and rusty, but still dependable. Of course, I don't actually drive it much these days, since I'm convinced that getting behind the wheel will be eventually, inevitably, disastrous.

*   *   *

The fact is, I can't stay away from cars when I'm heartbroken. Even when I tell myself I shouldn't drive, I end up hanging out at fancy used car lots, where they use terms like "vintage" and "pre-owned," just staring at those fine machines and dreaming about getaways.

A few days after Sandra left, I saw a 1956 vanilla-colored Porsche 356, the same kind of car in which Jimmy Dean spun right out of this world, and I swear I would have sold my mother to get it. But my mother's dead, Sandra was gone, and with her, every technological gadget I might ever have hocked for more than a hundred dollars, so I didn't have much with which to bargain with the devil, much less a car salesman. So I just balanced my two paper bags full of groceries and stared at the Porsche. I touched it a few times until, finally, one of the sales guys came out to the showroom and told me to go home. He said I looked like I was going to cry and offered to get me a cab, which he even paid for. That was very nice, but not as nice as driving myself would have been. The thing about cabs is that even if you're rich enough to pay the meter, they still have their limits.

And the idea after a break-up, of course, is to have no limits. I think that's why I like the notion of cars when I'm going through emotional angst. They provide this very cool, very American answer to pain: Even if you follow all the right directions from Chicago to San Francisco, all you need is one wrong turn—one little fuck-up—and you wind up in Mississippi, where there are no lesbians. It's so inevitable that you may as well enjoy the ride—the wind in your hair; the truck stop waitresses who've always been curious but have never been with other women other than in their fantasy letters about threesomes to *Penthouse Forum*; the radio blasting away with great rock 'n' roll songs, then great tear-jerking Country and Western songs, and then, when the tinny static stuff comes on while you're daredeviling through the swamps, you can always pop on a Philip Glass tape and think yourself really courageous.

I'm no fool, though. I know all this romantic posturing

about wide-open spaces, the adventurous South, and on-the-road possibilities; all these images and metaphors for freedom are inspired by men, jaded men like Jack Kerouac—that repressed homosexual who never really found love and died a pathetic mess of a human being. It's all a cover-up for just one thing: desperation.

I know from personal experience that, ultimately, no matter how many road maps I study, how many pairs of lacy underwear I pack for travel, how many times I tell myself that there are girls with Creole accents just waiting for me in New Orleans or Miami, all I'm going to do is drive around my ex-lover's house and have an accident. Sandra may pine for San Francisco, but she only lives one block away from me now. That's how crazy this is.

* * *

Of course, I've seen a therapist about this but all I remember is that she recommended I not see *Fatal Attraction*, which offended me terribly because, as a lesbian and a feminist, I would *never* resort to that sort of thing. Instead, I drive around and around and around Sandra's building, like a crazy wind-up toy that's *too* wound up and careens off into the furniture. I always want to throw up, but I don't—my stomach knots up and short-circuits the whole idea. It's like everything else about her and me: one false start after another.

We met through a mutual friend, a woman we were both crushed out on but who didn't want either of us. It took Sandra and me two dates to kiss, which is pretty typical by lesbian standards but a little slow by mine. By the time we made it to bed, it was more formality than desire: we already knew we were completely incompatible and went through it, I think, just so we could say we had.

Six months later we were both still prowling performing arts spaces and foreign movie houses as single lesbians. When we ran into each other again, we both seemed to glow with the right aura, kiss with lips that fit perfectly into each other's mouths, and make love with complementary rhythms. At first, even though it was very nice, I thought that it would be not a casual affair, but a *transient* relationship; I just wasn't sure we'd fall in love. But after another six months, even though I still had doubts about our romantic possibilities, she'd packed her little pointy boots, her Cuisinart, and her cats and re-settled them in my Uptown apartment.

That didn't quite work out, though. She wanted more closet space. She didn't like the posters I had on the walls. She thought my Mexican rugs were cheap. So after six months we moved into another apartment, one that was *ours* from the start, in which no decision could be made without the other's approval. It should have been suffocating, but it wasn't. There was a funny comfort, an uncanny understanding to the way our furniture fit together and our clothes began to match.

Of course, there still were little problems. I liked to stay up until the wee hours; she was up before dawn. I liked rock; she liked *salsa*. I liked sex in public places; she considered it an adventure to do it in our own kitchen. But slowly, almost imperceptibly, we began to behave in ways that said we wanted to be together for a long, long time: My clothes no longer rested on the exercycle, but got hung up at night; her dishes didn't sit for days but got washed as soon as she finished her meals. I opened a savings account; she named me as her spouse on her American Express and got me a card.

If life was too mundane to be heaven, it didn't matter; it was heaven on earth, or heaven enough. We had a long, train-like apartment with so much light we had to cover our eyes when we woke up. And on Sunday mornings, sitting in bed reading the paper while drinking coffee and soaking in Sandra's sleepy musk, I was as happy as I might ever have been.

It's true, I could never tell her about my weird Catholicism, or the way my heart hurt from pleasure sometimes, but I could confess to her my foulest fears, my most awful memories, and I knew they'd be safe. I don't know what she couldn't tell me, but I know no one had ever listened to her with quite the same rapture, or held her as fiercely when she was afraid. I know because she told me so, and to this day I believe her about these things.

All of that changed when Sandra took a business trip to San Francisco. She has told me what happened during that week a million times now, but even though I know too well how one thing led to another, I still don't see *how*—I don't understand why suddenly we didn't make sense, and why *they* did. She explained it by telling me she realized she wasn't in love with me anymore, and that she hadn't been for a long time. She talked about smoking cigarettes for the first time in years, and enjoying it; about walking on the beach; about going to bed at the same time every night with this new babe. She has told me far more than I ever wanted to know about what happened, but try as she might, she's been unable to make me understand how the gears stopped working for us, how the machinery went rusty without our knowing, and how one day the motor simply wouldn't turn over.

When it finally happened—when it became inevitable—I thought that, after five years together, the splitting would be agonizing. I worried about all the everyday things I might have lost sense of; I wondered, really, if I might not walk into walls or the middle of traffic, like a mental patient who thinks she wants freedom but really wants only to be out of the dark and into the light.

I feared the division of our possessions more than anything, not because they were so many but because they were so few and so precious. We were professionals, though, as efficient as the keenest of lawyers: cool, rational, shamelessly unsentimental. We went through the business of furniture without argument, and then we did the same with the dishes and kitchen appliances. After that, the few items of clothing that might have been debatable fell right into place with one or the other's wardrobe, almost as if they—and not we—knew instinctively where they belonged. Her CDs and my CDs gathered in perfect, separate piles.

Even the photo albums were simple to divide. We peeled back the plastic pages and plucked each image, one by one, laughing, and sometimes crying (actually, Sandra didn't cry; she hasn't cried once during this whole thing), remembering our trips to Santa Fe, and to Mexico City, and the good times in Tulsa. I was struck by how few pictures there were of *us*, but how many of her, standing beside this or that interesting tourist site; and of me, driving with that crazy look in my eyes, or leaning happily against the fender of a rented roadster. I always made us rent sports cars, no matter how inconvenient for luggage or sleeping, because there's nothing like driving at night, very fast, very sure, in a car that does absolutely everything you want it to. I think it's patriotic as hell. And I look corn-fed in those pictures, all of which she kept.

When I visit Sandra now, her cats eye me as if I were some long-lost relative, funny uncle, or divorced parent. It takes them a while to remember me, and I never know if they're reflecting her or acting on their own. I envy them nonetheless, their little brains, and that they get to sleep with her every night. The trouble is, most of the time—not all of the time, not when I'm out dancing with friends or watching TV—I still want her and our life back. I still want to go on long rides with her with the windows open, the radio blasting. I still want her to tell me stories, to fall asleep with her head in my lap while I drive. It's true that I didn't ever really know where we were going, but we *were* going, and it was steady, and it mattered. The trip itself was always as vital, as sunny, and as difficult as wherever we might end up.

Now, whenever I drive by, I look up at Sandra's apartment. I don't stare. I don't lunge out the window. I'm very subtle, the picture of calm. I check my gas gauge. I check my heat vents. I check my mirrors and hope no one has noticed that this is my millionth time around the block, and I'm wearing a groove into the street. Actually, I never have any idea of how many times I've gone around the block. I lose track; I *really* lose track. I get lost, not on the street but inside my own head. Then I get fucking terrified that someone will see me when I'm trying to be casual about checking my mirrors and that they won't believe me, they won't buy my act, and maybe they'll call the cops or the neighborhood crime watch.

I always imagine that I do it right, though: I reach outside the car to adjust my side view mirror, and then, right at that moment, I look up, casually of course, to see if Sandra's light is on, if the cats are poised on the window sill. I hope that maybe, just maybe, she'll pick that same moment to interrupt the flickering of the TV light with a few steps across the window frame, to the kitchen for more scotch or coffee, or to the bedroom to get her robe because it's cold and she misses me, or maybe, just maybe, to come to the damn window to look for me because she knows—I mean, she just absolutely *knows*—that I'm here, adjusting my mirrors outside her window, and needing her.

But, of course, it never works out that way. I don't see anything, or if I do it's all in a split second, an instant, that harrowing and fragile crack between the past and the future. I lose momentary control of the car, threaten the life of some neighborhood kid with the shrill of brakes and screaming car horns, and then drive as fast and far away as I possibly can—to the lake, to the Loop, to Kankakee—anywhere, just as long as I can hide my shame and panic when I get there.

❊ ❊ ❊

When Sandra first left, my friend Lourdes kept up my spirits by saying stupid things. "Women," she declared, cozy in the bosom of a seven-year relationship with a woman who is both a cook and a carpenter. "You can't live with 'em, and you can't live without 'em." I thought this was particularly insensitive of her, kind of arrogant actually, but so blatantly dumb that it never failed to get at least one demented, disgusted laugh out of me.

One day, as I contemplated buying materials for a hex to cause California to fall off the earth and thus eliminate all chances of happiness for Sandra and her new babe, Lourdes came up with what then seemed like an epiphany.

"You don't need any of this *santéria* stuff," she said. "You're a good egg; you just need a good chick to lay you."

I took her advice. I went on a sex binge, although it was difficult because I don't like to spend the night in a stranger's home, and I felt it was too soon to bring anybody to my home where the bed had been *our* bed, Sandra's and my cozy little love nest. So instead, I took girls out to Montrose Harbor, to the concrete circle that overlooks the lake and the best, most brilliant view of the city skyline. Even for natives, this can be breathtaking. We looked at the skyscrapers, at the long circuits of car lights on Lake Shore Drive, and at the way the sky divides into layers of blue and gray and pink, depending on the temperature, the pollution, and the cloud formations.

But instead of staring at clouds and trying to make sense of their shapes, we stared at the frozen waves and the little

20

pieces of ice—all looking suspiciously like California floating out into the ocean—and tried to make sense of the terribly awkward situation we had put ourselves in. Inevitably, though, we would make love in my VW, an idea I successfully sold to each girl with the promise of "lesbianizing" high school necking experiences.

The first time was pretty hard. I came up breathless, convinced that I was surely doomed, that whatever drool I was wiping off my chin had just sealed the absolute hopelessness of any potential recovery of my relationship with Sandra. I realized then that every time I closed my eyes, I kept hoping to open them to one of those safe Sunday mornings in bed with Sandra, our bodies tangled together, the cats on either side of us purring. I stared off into the darkness of the lake outside my car window, watched the rats skip between the fogged cars around us, and hyperventilated. I don't think I'd ever felt so alone in my life.

Then I noticed the girl I was with. I wish I could say I felt guilty for not remembering her until that moment, for having blanked her out so completely, but I didn't. Instead, I felt a kind of relief, a strange connection with all the other wretched souls of the earth—whether they were reckless macho men or women—who woke up from their own selfish pain and suddenly realized they were about to inflict it on an innocent bystander whose only desire was love, or comfort, or maybe even something as simple as fun.

When I finally looked at this girl, I didn't know what the hell was going on, but it was pretty clear that she didn't need or want to hear my hellish confessions. She was fine, suffering not one little shrapnel of guilt or regret, popping a tape into the VW's stereo, singing along, offering me more cheap wine. I wanted to say: *Don't you realize what we've just done?* But she just kept singing, perfectly at home there with her elbow in my stomach and my breast crushed by her shoulder.

I knew I'd hit bottom when I realized what I really wanted was to confess to Sandra what I'd done, and to beg forgiveness for this and any other transgression, real or imagined. I wanted to explain to the girl in my car that this could never, ever, happen again because, for heaven's sake, I was an unhappily-processing-my-primary-relationship-lesbian, and this, this thing that had just happened between us—which was, of course, beautiful and powerful and just plain great— was still, well, *adultery*. As soon as I dropped her off, I had every intention of going home to that long train-like apartment, kicking out any strangers who might have wandered in, and throwing myself at Sandra's mercy.

But I didn't say anything, and I didn't do anything either. I stared out the car window, thinking the city looked extraordinarily innocent, and eventually came to my senses. I moaned a few times, then forgave myself for the temporary insanity that let me forget the block of cozy bungalows that now exists between my mailbox and Sandra's, that we'd need marriage as a precondition for adultery, and that lesbians can only have, at best, a pseudo-marriage. I told the girl I was pseudo-separated, and surely headed for pseudo-divorce. Nonetheless, she never went out with me again, although she did buy me a scale model VW and attached a very charming note thanking me for helping her remember how much fun it used to be to park.

I've been back to Montrose Harbor numerous times since, but when I got her note I rubbed my tender muscles, climbed into my very real VW, and started doing circles around the block.

※　※　※

I know exactly when the accidents will happen. I also know that, short of being tossed around and bruised by the steering wheel and shoulder belt, I won't be seriously hurt. And I know, as sure as I know that when I find true love again I will forget all of this misery and dive head-first into it, that the next time—the very next time I get behind the wheel—I will experience my post-Sandra accident.

That's why I've been taking public transportation. It's why I've bought insurance—not in a conscientious way, but in a totally ignorant, sure-to-be exploited way. I simply filled out a form I found tucked into the weekly *Chicago Reader* and sent it off with a sixty-dollar down-payment to a company whose phone number spells I-N-S-U-R-E-D. I don't know what came over me; I just know that I needed insurance right there and then.

When I told Lourdes, she suggested that if I *know* the accident is imminent, and that if having the accident is the only way out of this post-Sandra depression, then maybe I need to just get it over with and run over a newspaper boy, ruin a mailbox, or hit a station wagon filled with suburbanites. She said that maybe by avoiding the accident I'm delaying the healing process, sidestepping the very idea that Sandra and I are as dead as disco.

Just yesterday I went over to Sandra's—an official visit to drop off a few things she'd forgotten in the move (a bottle of contact lens solution, a box of postcards, and a couple of pairs of cotton panties, all carried over in a paper grocery bag)—and for a few minutes everything seemed fine between us. We hugged when I arrived and, although she seemed smaller in my arms than ever before, her skin was as familiar and painful as ever.

Still, we talked without effort, laughed without embarrassment. It was almost like old times. Then the phone rang. Even before Sandra's answering machine picked it up, we both knew it was San Francisco calling. We stood there, listening to the whir of the tape, the click, and then the voice that has replaced mine at those times when only whispers matter.

I know I was lucky: Sandra picked up the phone and very carefully said she'd call back in a bit, that we were chatting. She could have gloated; she could have smirked; she could have laughed nervously. All of that might have fit. But she didn't. She did everything the sensitive-relationship manuals say to do: She exhibited patience, grace, and even gave me a little squeeze on the arm and a wet little peck on my cheek. She looked as sad and understanding as if she were my best friend, not the woman who'd dumped me. There was no question in my mind she was *trying*.

But it didn't matter. I'd already clenched my teeth, my fists, all of my muscles, and there was nothing that could loosen them up again.

I still haven't been able to get the episode out of my mind. And that's the part I don't understand. I know I've accepted the situation. I know that to go back would require a blinding absolution on both our parts, of which we're both totally incapable. I'm not asking for another chance. I've accepted we're over. I've even accepted, on some deep and awful level, that we are and will be with others. What I want is an answer of another sort: How long will this nag at me? How long will it hurt?

＊　＊　＊

I've decided to take Lourdes's advice again, so I'm driving my car and looking for trouble. I'm listening to new tapes, tapes I bought on a lark at the 7-Eleven around the corner from my apartment. The place was blazing in fluorescence, humming right along when I went in, moved aside the little American flags that hung from the shelves, and picked out every third tape across the top row. I wound up with some heavy metal, Loretta Lynn, and a collection of the Archies greatest hits, but I will survive all of their flaws and find beauty in them if it kills me.

My new insurance card is in the back pocket of my jeans. I've got a tall, cool take-out Coke between my legs, and I'm pressing down on the accelerator and singing along whenever possible with Metallica. I'm in complete control. I pass a Jeep on Montrose Avenue, right at the intersection with Broadway, and leave behind a mess of pedestrians waving their fists in the air. At Marine Drive I shift and laugh, sending a man in a raincoat chasing after his frightened dog on the perfect lawn around Lake Shore Drive. I'm in the fourth lane and my radio is so damn loud I can't hear my own voice singing along. My hair whips all over my face, a crazy dance of snakes. Before I know it, I'm leaning hard, away from the S-curve, rounding up to the Loop, and I realize I'm running out of prime city concrete.

I'm thinking, yeah, the interstate looks good, and I change lanes and climb the entrance ramp off Lake Shore Drive to I-55, pumping the VW, sure that everything I need will be taken care of in a matter of miles, even before the tape turns itself over. I'm thinking, yeah, San Francisco; I could drive there in a straight line if I wanted to. I'm thinking all this, thinking crazy, murderous thoughts when everything— absolutely everything—comes to a dead halt right there on the entrance ramp, right there in front of me, in one overwhelming wall of excruciating sound and light. I feel my head graze the windshield, like some kind of slow-motion heavenly knocking—immediate and exquisite and over with before I know what's actually happened.

But I'm fine, and nothing has happened. Nothing, that is, except that the belt has practically cut my shoulder with the sheer force of how I descended on the brakes, all one hundred and twenty pounds of me, as soon as I saw the red lights going wild in front of my face. I stopped on a dime—*on a dime*. The guy behind me landed on his horn, releasing one long, petulant whine. I sneered at him in the mirror but he threw his hands in the air to apologize, and I realized I had to forgive him, I had no other choice. The guy behind him, I'm sure, kissed his bumper. I don't know after that. I look in the mirror again, but there's no sign of the end to this loose, dangerous train of cars on the ramp, all stopped for god knows what.

I jerk on the emergency brake, unbuckle, rub my shoulder, and leap out of the VW to find, literally, less than an inch between me and the car in front of me, a black BMW from which a gaggle of preschoolers improbably scatters. There are lights everywhere: red and terrible white lights from all the cars, blue lights threatening epileptic seizures from a cop car that's backing up on the shoulder of the interstate. I try to cover my eyes from all the glare and notice a stream of liquid running between my shoes and down the ramp's incline: green anti-freeze, water maybe, with a thread of something vivid and red that looks like blood. My shoes are soaked with it before I can move.

I walk up, maneuvering from small child to small child, all of them curious and straining to get a look at what's under the wheel of the BMW. A woman's voice tells them not to look, causing every one of them to stare even more intently. "Wow," says one, his eyes as wide as saucers. "Disgusting," says another, her face greenish. A man in a dark trench coat is pacing right in front of the car. "Oh my god," he says. "Oh my god," over and over and over again. He has a perfect haircut and his lower lip curls like he's about to cry. I can't see anything except that the liquid flowing down the concrete ramp is almost black now. The lights are so bright, and everything's so confusing.

"Did the dog belong to anybody here?" asks one of the cops, averting his gaze from the scene of the crime.

I look at the colossal, mangled heap under the BMW's wheel and make out a blondish mutt, one eye like blue glass, the other black with blood from the ruptured sclera. His huge body is torn apart, and he looks like the devil. He's wearing no tags, no collar, nothing. His hair is soaked with dirt and all the liquids pouring from the car's engine.

"It's my dog," I lie, reaching out tentatively to the still warm paw, as open as a catcher's mitt.

"Well, what was he doing on the highway?" asks the same cop. "How come he doesn't have a collar? I mean, I'm really sorry and everything but...jesus...you got any identification, huh?"

I pat my jacket for my wallet, not finding it, finally reach back to my jeans pocket, pull out my insurance card, and hand it to the cop. His partner, as faceless as he is, directs traffic around my bug and the BMW. Since I'm squatting, the headlights blaze right into my face, and for an instant I feel like a criminal caught in some horrible act. One of the preschoolers, a little girl with a stammer, tells me she's real sorry her dad ran over my dog. I just stare at her, and she backs off, bumping right into the cop.

"You know this won't pay for the dog, right?" the cop says, handing me back my insurance card. "I mean, you're still responsible for whatever damage to his car, but I don't think you can get anything on the dog."

"She's irreplaceable," I tell him, and let go of the demon mutt's paw. I stand up and cover my eyes. The cop, who thinks I'm crying, squeezes my shoulder.

Now the cop's partner is in the squad car, making noises on the police radio. The squad's blue lights keep going around and around and around. The man in the trench coat, who can't seem to meet my eyes, keeps apologizing to me. "I'm sorry; I'm really sorry," he says, biting his lip until it finally bleeds. I squeeze his shoulder, and we make out a police report together. I think I'm going to owe him some money, but he says no, that he killed my dog, that he can't take my money for what little damage the dog may have done to his car. We're talking hundreds, maybe thousands of dollars here, but he insists.

Just my luck, I think, I've stumbled upon the last Good Samaritan in the universe, and driving a BMW no less. I can barely keep from laughing.

※　※　※

When I get back in the VW, I check my emergency brake, my gas gauge, then I look in the mirror. My face is smudged and wet, a strange combination of dirt, sweat and, maybe, tears. I really don't know. I sit in silence for a while, just watching the cars go around me and the BMW. I watch them disappear, not so much into the flow of traffic as into the night, beyond the slope of I-55, into the long line of boarded-up houses and old factories, neglected lawns, and loose dogs around the interstate.

I remember seeing Sandra for the first time, dressed in black, somber, and a little scared, and making her laugh. I have no idea what it was I said. It's all behind me now.

Eventually, a huge blue city truck pulls up, followed by a tow truck. The city workers, all men with rough voices whose breath I can see, scrape the dog from under the BMW and hook the car to the tow truck. They hose down the concrete as the man in the trench coat and his family climb into a taxi. Before the taxi's off the ramp, the water has frozen, and workers are sprinkling salt over it. Finally, it's just me and the cops on the ramp. They turn off their blue lights, flick on their turn signal, and wait for me to mainstream into traffic.

The Cradleland

I was still standing, my pants pushed midway down my thighs. I took her in my arms. That's all I did. I took her in my arms and kissed her, holding my breath the whole time, then said something—I don't know what—that I meant as thanks but which sounded more like a gurgle. She turned away from me, flinging her hair from her face, and laughed, stroked my cheek once and walked out of the bathroom stall.

My belt buckle, dangling, clicked against the porcelain. I could hear the water running at the sink, the flow muffled by her hands rubbing underneath it. Then *swoosh*, off. I heard her heeled shoes clickety clack across the tiled floor. Paper towels flapping like wings. The door hissing shut. I swore I heard her sigh as she disappeared into the great commuter masses at the train station.

I finally let out my breath, all at once, perhaps too fast, too soon, and collapsed against the stall door. I wound my fingers around the coat hook. *Wow.* It's all I could think of. I'm sure if someone had taken my picture it would have shown me out of focus because of the trembling, thighs shiny, mouth all red, maybe drooling, eyes wide and fantastic, looking something like a victim, but way too ecstatic. *Wow.*

■ ■ ■

I had been telling my new girlfriend, Sylvia, about this last night, but it was just a fantasy then. We'd been wrapped up under the covers, our breaths little hot jets, then normal. We were just messing around, sharing fantasies. She told me hers of doing it on a Ferris wheel, and I decided to shut up and not mention that I'd already done it that way. I got dizzy from the memory of the lights and my fear of falling. Then, since we were on the subject of sex, we decided to talk about more serious matters, like AIDS and risk and all that stuff that nobody ever really wants to talk about but which is de rigueur nowadays.

We're a relatively new relationship—just a couple of weeks—and we're still getting some of the details out of the way, like HIV status, the names of each other's brothers and sisters, and where we went to college. So Sylvia told me about the last time she'd had unsafe sex, when a rubber broke while her ex-boyfriend had his cock up her ass. Sylvia's story depressed me terribly, even though she'd been tested and was negative, because it was essentially my roommate, Tomás's, story, and he was dying. Plus, when I'd met Sylvia, I'd been hoping that for the first time in years I'd find a partner who was so low at risk we could actually get up close and exchange bodily fluids.

For the record, I'm fine. I mean, I've never been with a boy, and just before the epidemic started raging I went through a long period of celibacy. Since then, I've practiced safe sex as a matter of course. I rationalize it this way: It's easier just to have safe sex, at least initially, than to go through that awkward clinical dialogue to determine if it's necessary. I figure that later, after we get close, it'll be easier to talk. Besides, I've promised myself I won't hold HIV status against anybody, and so, to guard against my own prejudice, I just play safe and ask questions later. I figure that if I really like somebody, it'll be too late to back out of actually admitting it to myself.

So, basically, I'm at *no* risk. But after Sylvia told me her story about the broken rubber we decided we'd just stay on the safe sex diet until she gets another test, about six months down the road. And if we're still together then, we'll just guzzle each other up.

To my surprise, Sylvia was willing to drop the restrictions right after our little talk—convinced that, lesbian sex being what it is, the chances of actual transmission were so low we were probably safe anyway. But with a fresh mental picture of an increasingly sicker and bed-ridden Tomás, like a half-blind chick with its red mouth open, struggling to get out of the nest, I said no. I said we'd have to wait.

* * *

Tomás, besides being my roommate, is my best friend. We've been living together since we both graduated from Stevens College, a tiny school with a student population of seven hundred and fifteen in the middle of Nowheresville, Indiana. We both picked it because it had a good English department, offered us lots of scholarship money, and isn't far from either of our repulsive little hometowns. When I met him, Tomás felt the need to travel back and forth every weekend because his high school sweetheart—some seriously Christian girl with whom he obviously didn't have to prove anything sexual—was still a senior and he, struggling mightily to stay in the closet, figured he'd escape into heterosexual marriage as soon as possible.

I wasn't in a much better place. My hometown sweetie was a junior whom I'd deliberately picked because he was younger and so underdeveloped. But in the summer between my high school graduation and arrival on campus, he'd had a growth spurt and a hormonal charge. Suddenly he was very tall, had grown a prickly moustache, and was getting erections all over the place. For a while I considered having oral sex with him. I thought it might be an easy way to keep him around without risking pregnancy or actually having to do *it*.

But when he pulled his cock out of his pants and dropped it in my hands, I found the silkiness of its skin deceiving—a denial of its power and danger—and I couldn't bring it to my mouth.

Mercifully, pretty much upon meeting, Tomás and I promptly dropped our hometown hang-ups and took up with each other. Together we had banter and fun, a solid study partnership, respect and refuge. In many ways, we were perfect together. Not that we acknowledged why we were interested in one another. That took about six months.

* * *

It was on a lark that we went to The Gold Star, an Indianapolis drag bar Tomás's frat brothers thought might be an adventure. The brothers—all faceless now—had heard of the place from one of the older guys and decided to check it out. It was pretty cheesy—lots of weird tinsel, what looked like Christmas lights, several blinding disco balls, and queens who seemed as colorful and magically out of place as tropical birds.

None of us had been to a drag show before or had any idea what to expect. At first, I was afraid the frat guys would get boisterous and defensive and have to prove their manhood or something, but once we entered, a strange kind of silence fell over them. The music was very loud, but that wasn't what caused it. And the place was packed, but that wasn't it either.

We were seated ringside, with an unobstructed view of the stage and even a glimpse of the wings where, on closer inspection, the queens seemed more like men in women's clothing than the women they were trying to project. They held their bodies differently in the shadows than in the light. Less loose. More angular. Impatient. I don't know what it was.

One by one, the queens came out to the brilliant spot-

34

light, their manners exaggerated and glittery. One of them resembled Elizabeth Taylor, complete with mole and what looked from our table like violet eyes. Another looked like Farrah Fawcett, who was so popular then, with her hair cascading in waves to her shoulders. They lip-synched along to records, usually something torchy like "What I Did for Love" (big fave) or "The Man That Got Away." Everyone in the room knew the words and eventually sang along. Tomás and I looked at each other, then we both dropped our eyes in the same flickering instant.

While the queens mouthed lyrics, big beefy guys stepped up and, with what I was sure were sticky fingers, curled dollar bills into make-believe cleavages, immaculately manicured hands, hip-high boots, hot pants waistbands—whatever. The ritual was understood and expected, and Tomás and I were amazed. We looked on, transfixed, amateur anthropologists having stumbled upon an eerie, ancient, and enchanted world.

I did notice on this initial visit to The Gold Star that there were very few women in the club, and even fewer whom I might identify, by whatever means, as lesbians. Most of the women there had very heterosexual seeming male escorts who held them close, or put their arms around them as if to protect them. There was much laughter, and I remember thinking how sad it all was.

Those women who did look like dykes were pretty stereotypical—square-bodied, tough-looking. I noticed one of them staring at me, and I looked back for a moment, then immediately dropped my arm around Tomás's shoulder in an awkward and inadvertent reversal of what I'd seen the heterosexuals do. She wore leather, had her thumb hooked into her jeans pocket, and raised up her beer to me as if to toast. I was flustered and looked away, afraid that perhaps I was being recognized as one of *them*—an idea that titillated as much it terrified me.

A week later, I went to the bar by myself. I hung out on the periphery and in the corners, scrutinizing every face that came near me and hoping to stay invisible, like a bat in the rafters. It took me hours to realize I'd come looking for the woman who'd lifted her beer in my direction. When it hit me, I crossed my arms on my chest and started to leave, muttering, "excuse me" without looking up as I bumped and pushed against the bodies lining the way out of the bar. Suddenly a familiar hand curled its fingers around my elbow and tugged; I jerked. When I turned around, I fell into Tomás's arms. Behind him were a handful of his new friends, all singing along to "My One and Only."

* * *

Sylvia's lying on her side, stroking my back. Her nails, which I never feel when her hand's inside me, are like feathers now, causing me chills. "I have to get up," she whispers, kissing the back of my neck. All the soft little hairs stand on end at her touch.

"Nobody's stopping you," I tease. She moves her knee up against me so that her thigh comes right up and presses into me. I press back. I'm wet.

I know this is dangerous. This kind of comfort, so easy and familiar at the beginning, can become weighty later. Already, in the first couple of weeks we've spent together, Sylvia has been late to work almost every morning. Not because of some raging heat but because of this warmth. Later, when she gets in trouble at the office and the cuddling's old hat, I know she'll resent it.

"Hey, come on, get up," I say, trying to hold off the future. I turn around, kiss her quickly, and push her away from me.

"All right," she mutters. "I'm up, I'm up." But she's not.

Instead, she lowers her head under the sheets and covers my nipple with her mouth. I grit my teeth, not because it isn't wonderful, but because I'm trying not to moan. I'm trying really hard to be disciplined, to resist temptation. "Sylvia," I groan, and although she makes some noise in response, I know she isn't listening.

Eventually, she hops up, grabs clean underwear from an open drawer, and jumps into the shower. I stay in bed, listening to the sound of the water, the way the rush of it varies as she moves underneath it. I know that if I don't get up right here and now, I'll lie in bed all morning.

I can script it from here: the headlong rush into feelings and more feelings, the sense of awe (even though we've been here before), then that abrupt moment of discovery—something similar, I'm sure, to what Montezuma must have felt upon learning that Córtez was not a god, but a man—that moment when we will realize (as we must) that this is fine, for now, but nothing more.

"You're wasting daylight," Sylvia says, wet and shivering from her shower. Her body is covered with goose bumps. "You're just too tempting." She yanks the sheets from around me, grabs my ankles, and drops my legs over the side of her futon. "If you don't get up, I'll never get out of here," she says. "Don't you have things to do?"

"Too many," I say, pulling myself into a sitting position. For starters, I have to check in on Tomás, with whom I've been spending less and less time. "I have to see what the disease of the day is at my house," I say, suddenly surprised and embarrassed at how bitter I sound.

Sylvia stands in front me and puts her fingers on a couple of pressure points on my neck. "You're tense," she says, and kisses my forehead as her fingers work on my muscles.

I close my eyes, not to relax, but because she's beautiful, and it's too painful to look.

When Tomás first got sick, he got what seemed like every opportunistic disease associated with AIDS: tiny zits that became huge rashes, major thrush, syphilis, something that looked like mold all over the bottom of his feet, constant bouts of pneumonia, and really bad periodontal infections. His breath was like sulfur. Some days, if there hadn't been too much traffic in and out of his room, it hung in the air like a toxic cloud.

Now Tomás mostly just lies there, too weak to read, wheezing in this horribly slow, stingy way. We light sage in his room. His breath is too slight to smell anyway, but I suspect if I could smell it, it'd be muskier now. Maybe I'm just used to it, I don't know.

"Where is Charles II when you need him?" Tomás whispers. He wears his glasses in bed. They make his head seem larger and more square, like the head of a famine victim. "I need to shave off my hair, to wear a huge, powdered periwig. I want to be buried in something with ruffles, laces, and ribbons."

I don't say anything. I remember him back in college, hanging around the dressing room at The Gold Star, telling the queens how to use their accessories—how to swing their shiny purses; when in a song to stop and touch their faux pearls; how to toss their scarves with authority. I never understood why Tomás stayed on the sidelines, never taking the stage himself. Now I just smile and pat the lump in the bed that corresponds to his hand.

"Look at nature: It's always the males who are glorious, massive, and colorful," he says, closing his eyes. His nostrils are crusty. "Boy lions have their manes. Boy chickens have combs and wattles and fluff. And what about that outrageous cock of the rock with his wild orange pompadour, huh?"

And I'm thinking, yeah, but it's the girl lions who kill, and it's the girl birds who lay the eggs. So why do I feel so useless?

* * *

What I told Sylvia was that I wanted to be ravished. After I explained everything—that I wanted the encounter to be anonymous, that it had to be in a public place, that I wanted to resist, and that I never wanted to see the other woman again—she told me I was confused.

"You want to be raped," she said, disgusted. "You can't want to be raped."

"I don't want to be *raped*," I said. "I want to be taken."

"Against your will?"

"Well, a little against my will," I admitted.

"That's like being a little pregnant," she said, clearly frustrated.

"It's a fantasy, Syl," I said. "The same rules don't apply."

"I'm worried about you," she said, then turned on her side with her back to me.

We stayed like that in the dark for a few minutes until, finally, I molded my body around hers. She was a little stiff at first, but eventually relaxed and pushed back against me so that the fabric of her slip rubbed lazily against my bare stomach. She groped behind her, meaning, I think, to stroke me with her free hand, but instead of feathers her nails felt like little claws this time. I wanted to get a glass of water and to pee, but I didn't want to move either, afraid whatever I did would have meaning well beyond my actual gestures.

"I can't rape you," she said in a whisper that sounded both frightened and wistful.

I pulled her closer. "I don't want you to rape me."

"I can't *ravish* you either," she said. "I can't do anything like that. It's completely beyond me."

I sighed. "Honey, relax, it's a fantasy," I said. "It's not about you." Then I felt her stiffen again, and her body peeled away from me in an instant, as if her slip were a layer of skin, blistering.

*　*　*

"Se te olvida/ que me quieres a pesar de lo dices."
When I get home, Tomás's mother is visiting. Mostly, I like Virginia, twice married, twice widowed, and still looking. She's washing a sink full of socks and singing along with Olga Guillot, who croons from the stereo speakers. When Virginia sees me, she holds up her wet and soapy hands as if she were a doctor emerging from surgery and beckons me for a kiss.

"How is he?" I ask, and she just shrugs. They have the same shrug, I think (even though Tomás doesn't shrug much anymore): they lean their heads to the right, as if they're trying to make their ears touch their shoulders.

"Pues llevamos en el alma cicatrices/imposibles de borrar," Virginia sings to the socks, submerging her hands once more in the sink. "What can I tell you?" she says to me, then shrugs again.

The second to the last time I saw Tomás shrug like that was when he came back from a business trip to San Francisco about a year and a half ago. He'd had an adventure, he told me, a crazy weekend fling with a beautiful boy he'd met in the cookbook section of a bookstore. "I feasted for two days and nights, feasted as if in Valhalla," he had said, grinning.

It wasn't until later that he told me he'd had anal sex for the first time in five years, and that he knew exactly when the boy's rubber had broken, but knew, too, that it was too late. He said he didn't stop, but rather tightened his legs around the boy's waist.

The last time I saw Tomás shrug like that, like his mother

40

just did in our kitchen, was when he got diagnosed with HIV a few months later. "I'm not hanging around," he said. "I'm not going to drag this out from here to eternity. I'm going to live my life, and then I'm going to drop dead."

We didn't cry—we barely even hugged. Instead, we put Madonna's "Like a Prayer" on the stereo, cranked it up as loud as it would go, then danced and danced around our apartment like cranes in the wild, our arms out, knees up, eyes wide open.

"*Se te olvida/que hasta puedo hacerte mal si me decido,*" Virginia sings sadly, and points to her son's bedroom door with her chin. Some months back, when his vision was still sharp, Tomás read that goldfinch were considered protection against the plague during the Dark Ages, and he put a little picture of one on his door. Most of his visitors misunderstood—and Tomas didn't explain, or didn't make sense when he explained—and people just thought he'd developed a thing for birds, so they brought over all sorts of drawings and photos. Soon his door became covered with images of toucans and blackburnian warblers and flamingos and, of course, Tomás's favorite—the cock of the rock, a flaming orange South American bird with feathers swept as high as Conway Twitty's hair.

"*Pues tu amor lo tengo muy comprometido—*" I drop my coat and head for Tomás's room. "*...Pero a fuerza/no será.*"

"Howya doin'?" I ask Tomás, taking a seat on the chair next to his bed. I smell the sage burning on his dresser. His eyes are a little more yellowish than usual, as if there's some sort of film over them.

"My body's like Africa at the beginning of time," he says in a barely audible whisper. "The cradleland, I'm housing a most impressive roster of protozoa fungi bacteria single-celled parasites, all kinds of free-living organisms, I'm the Nile, I'm Cleopatra herself."

41

He talks in a rush, practically without punctuation. For an instant I'm afraid he's going to choke.

"I feel so light today," Tomás says. "My bones are empty."

I want to tell him about aerodynamics, about the way a hollow skeleton helps birds fly, but at that moment Virginia steps into the room and asks if I'll give her a ride to the train station. "It's starting to snow," she says, standing at the bedroom door, her hands still soapy and outstretched. I can hear the water still running in the kitchen sink.

Tomás closes his eyes, makes an attempt to move his hand from under the covers. "Don't take too long," he tells me. His eyebrow twitches. Virginia stands at the door for a moment, confused. Then she shrugs.

As I wait for Virginia to say good-bye to Tomás, I stand by the front door and check my key chain for the car key, the front door key, the apartment key. I count the change in my pocket, ascertain that I've got my cash card, my Visa, my driver's license, then realize I'm also carrying a photograph of my first lover, a half-Arab, half-Welsh women's studies instructor from my college days. I realize she has a remarkable resemblance to Sylvia.

※　※　※

I didn't plan it. I dropped off Virginia at the train station, realized the traffic was only going to get worse because of the snow, and knew that I needed to piss before I drove home. I threw the car next to the curb right under the L tracks, noticing a bird's nest stuffed into the joint where the girders met. As I rushed to the station—convinced my bladder might explode—I heard behind me the fluttering of birds. I turned to look, but by the time I pinpointed them, they were just black dots disappearing into the white cover of snow.

Inside the train station rest room, the walls melted into

the floor, all small white tiles with occasional spots of baby blue tiles where damage had been repaired. It was cavernous, with cathedral-like ceilings and larger-than-life mirrors above the sinks. The fixtures were metal and glistening. Everything smelled of ammonia. When I entered, my running shoes made a kind of muffled sound.

I stopped when I saw her, a woman in a business suit, her purse dangling from her shoulder by a thin, tasteful leather band. She was taller than me, more graceful, too blond to appeal to me under normal circumstances. She was leaning into her reflection, fixing her mascara. Then she measured me through the mirror with one of those dismissive, angry looks.

I immediately turned, flushed red, faced the stalls, and pushed the first door open. Like a boy, I confronted the toilet, confused, then turned around, fumbled with my belt. I undid my buckle, took a deep breath. Then I saw her through the crack between the door and the hinges, coming, it seemed, toward the stalls. I panicked, convinced she was just outside the door. I looked down and saw her feet, then *whack*. Her hand pushed against the door. I double-checked the lock, clutched at my belt. Her dark blue shadow drifted past. I heard a stall door opening, shutting, a click. Fabric rustling, small pieces of metal clashing. My pulse was pumping.

I continued to stand, wondering if I'd just imagined the whole thing—the way she'd glared at me through the mirror, the way she'd hit the door of my stall. In the background, I heard the steady stream of her pee into the toilet. I wanted to look to see which way her feet were pointing, but I couldn't move. *Flush.*

I had just dropped my pants, bent my knees, and started to piss, when—*slam*—she appeared again, popping the lock on the suddenly open door, then leaning down toward me, her hand reaching for the current between my legs. My mouth dropped. Her fingers penetrated me so hard and so effortlessly that for an instant she lifted me off my feet. I floundered, unable to protest, watching the piss run warm all over her hand, my thighs. I felt a wetness around my ankle. I grabbed at her, trying to regain my balance. Every time my buckle hit something it was like a bell ringing. Then I shuddered, and held her, tighter.

"You forget/that you love me in spite of what you say.
"We carry scars in our hearts/impossible to erase.
"You forget/that I can do you harm if I should choose to.
"Your love is mine/but not against your will."

From "La Mentira" ("The Lie") by Alvaro Carrillo, 1965.

Above All, A Family Man

M y name is Tommy Drake, and I'm dying. This is no delusion or attention-getting device; enough doctors have figured it out, and I believe them. I've got the cough, the nausea, the swollen glands—I even have a few of those splotches. Luckily, you can't really see them, although there's one on my neck that's starting to spread. I don't have much in the way of material possessions—an old Pioneer stereo, a few sticks of furniture, and a backpack full of clothes—but I did make out a will leaving it all to a not-for-profit group in Chicago, which is my hometown.

Right now I'm speeding down Interstate 55, stretched flat on the passenger's seat and rubbing my stomach, which is taut on the outside but queasy on the inside. I rub it in a circular motion, with my hand under my shirt, but it doesn't help much. My hand just gets warm, and it feels as primitive and interminable as scratching flint for fire. Nothing happens, except that everything keeps turning inside me.

"You okay?" asks Rogelio, who's driving at rocket speed. I know he's doing more than eighty miles an hour, but every time I say something he tells me he's just a little bit above the speed limit. Even from my reclining position (I'm so low my headrest is bumping the back seat), I can see those big trucks blinking as we zoom past them, but he just tells me to relax.

I try to explain that I'm nauseous and wish he'd slow down, especially around the curves, but my mouth is too dry. My tongue is a beached whale, swollen and sticky. What comes out is a pathetic peep that makes Rogelio laugh. He pats my thigh with rough affection, turns up the radio, and presses his foot on the gas pedal. My body pushes against the car seat from the acceleration.

"Slow down," I finally manage to say.

"What?"

"Goddamn it, slow down!" I'm screaming now, and my throat can't take it; I start to cough, the force of it pitching me from side to side.

"I can't hear you," he says, lowering the volume. He glances at me, then turns back to the road. "What did you say?"

I want to hit him, but all I can do is wipe the drool from my chin. I have my cuffs undone, and my sleeve flaps up to my face, which is now sweaty and red. "Slow down," I say. "Please."

"Okay, okay," he says with exaggerated reassurance. "You take it easy, okay?"

I nod and close my eyes, settling back on the seat and feeling the weight of the car as Rogelio slowly pumps the brake. He reaches across to open my window a little. As he turns the handle, his arm brushes against me, just at my stomach, and I lift my shirt. On its way back to the steering wheel, his hand pats my stomach, which is the wrong thing to do. My insides slosh around, and I swallow. Then I angrily force his hand flat on my abdomen and just hold it there against his will. I don't want to get sick; I don't want to die.

"We're almost in St. Louis," he says, freeing his hand. "You ever been to St. Louis?"

"No," I say. "But I've driven past it."

"You seen the Arch?"

"From the road." I reach up and feel my head for fever, but I'm suddenly fine. "What's in St. Louis besides the Arch?"

"Nothing," Rogelio says with a laugh.

I think he must never stop when he gets behind the wheel.

It's just a straight line to him, point A to point B—no bathroom stops, no meals, nothing. "I want to stop in St. Louis," I say.

Rogelio laughs because he thinks I'm kidding. His laugh is almost a giggle, kind of high-pitched. There's a girlishness to it, but if anybody ever pointed it out, he'd probably never laugh again.

"I'm serious, I want to stop in St. Louis."

He's still smiling. "Well, we'll get gas there, okay?"

"No, no, I want to stop, to get off the road."

He does a double-take, but I just grin up at him. "Why? Are you getting sick?" he asks.

"No, actually, I'm feeling okay right now."

"Tommy, we can get to Tulsa tonight, but if we stop in St. Louis, we'll waste time," he says. "Besides, there's nothing in St Louis. If there was, I would have heard about it by now, don't you think?"

Rogelio is a dark, handsome motherfucker with Indian hair and cheekbones as sharp as a razor. Now he's giving me this insinuating smile, this man-of-the-world macho look.

"I want to get off the road," I say, smiling back. "I want to see the Arch."

"The Arch?" He whines, his face all wrinkled up. "We'll be late. What about your friends in Santa Fe?"

"Rogelio, at the speed you're driving, we'll be in Santa Fe in an hour. Anyway, I can always call them."

My friends are Paul and Ron, these two guys who run a gallery in Santa Fe. It's very Southwest but very gay at the same time. That means they have buffalo skulls like every other Santa Fe gallery, but they also show glossy Mapplethorpe prints of boys in leather. Ron and I were lovers about ten years ago, and we've remained friends. When I told him the news, he and Paul invited me to stay with them, a kindness I'll never get to repay.

49

Rogelio isn't at all happy. He's actually pouting because of my request. "You'd deny me my *last* chance to see the St. Louis Arch?" I ask. It's a guilt trip, I know, but I do want to get off the road. And it's true, too. If that Arch and I are ever going to get together—not that it would ever have occurred to me before—this is our last chance Texaco.

"No, Tommy, I wouldn't deny you," Rogelio says, and it's with genuine feeling. Because he thinks he's treated me badly, he kind of sinks in the driver's seat. The perk is that his foot lightens up on the gas pedal, and we begin to approach the speed limit.

There is, however, an irony in his response. The fact is that Rogelio denies me pretty routinely. Not pleasures, mind you. He's generous by nature, and he'll do most anything, especially for me. And frankly, it's not because of what I do for him; I'm nothing special. I'm okay. I'm kind of cute, actually. But that has nothing to do with it.

* * *

Rogelio picked me for no reason other than that I spoke a little Spanish to his kids. He's got four of them, at least that I know of. Two boys, two girls, ages four to twelve. They're little brown butterballs, all of them overweight. At the Montrose Street beach where I met them, they practically bounced around Rogelio. They were playing a loose game of soccer when the oldest boy kicked the ball right into my lap, knocking the newspaper out of my hands. I was pissed off, and ready to say something mean, but then I saw Daddy, and that changed things.

Oh, it wasn't lightning or love at first sight. It was simple fear. Rogelio is as sinewy as tire tread: every ligament is perfectly outlined. And there he was, this little bull ready to charge if I said the wrong thing. So I resurrected some high school Spanish and told his kid to be careful next time, that I'd been sitting in my beach chair all morning in the same spot, and I'd appreciate it if they'd play somewhere else. Rogelio and I never took our eyes off each other, but the look was as much an invitation to murder as to love.

Montrose Beach is a small peninsula that juts out into Lake Michigan. It offers a pretty amazing view of the Loop, Lake Shore Drive snaking north, and the park along the water's edge. But for me, the best part is that Montrose is not a gay beach. That is, it's a respite. The folks there are mostly Latinos and Asians, usually in family groups. The kids play soccer or volleyball; the young men wear long pants and smoke a lot of cigarettes while the women keep an eye on things. For the most part, I'm left alone. I can read, think, just hang out, with very little chance of distraction. If I really want to cruise, all I have to do is walk down to the rocks on Belmont Avenue, and there are boys of all colors everywhere.

So when Rogelio stared back hard, this was a surprise. His roly-poly wife was sitting on a beach towel not too far from us, and I could tell she wasn't happy about any of this. She yelled something at him—I think it was to be careful—and he retreated, kicking the ball back to his kids. I'm sure she meant to say she just didn't want him to get in trouble threatening a white man, but I'd bet her real reasons were different.

"It's okay," I said in her direction, my eyes still fixed on Rogelio but softer now. He smiled shyly, which was so unexpected, I laughed. Then he puffed up, offended, his manhood on the line—it was as if I'd guessed about that high-pitched sound, and he was terrified.

He stomped over. "What's so funny?" he asked, surprising me again. Unlike most of the other people on Montrose Beach, Rogelio speaks English fairly well. He has an accent, but it's slight, more endearing than anything else. "Are you laughing at my wife?"

"No," I said, "I'm laughing at you."

He stepped back. "What?"

"You're making a big deal out of nothing," I said. "Your kids were careless. I told them to be careful, and now your wife is trying to protect you from the big, bad gringo."

"I think you're trying to embarrass me in front of my family," he said quite seriously.

"I think you're crazy," I told him. "I don't even know you."

He winced in the hot sun, jets of black hair breezing around his face. "If you're worried about that," he said, "we can meet here tomorrow morning, at eight o'clock."

His eye contact made it clear this wasn't a challenge to a duel, not in the usual sense. "The beach doesn't open until nine."

"Exactly." His face was stern.

"All right," I said, thinking the whole thing mighty amusing and that I'd never actually meet him.

"Okay," he said, his muscles finally loosening. Then he smiled. "How big are you?"

I looked at him incredulously. I mean, you read about this kind of stuff, but does it ever really happen? "What kind of a question is that?" I asked him. "And in front of your wife."

"Well?"

It was my turn to feel embarrassed. "How big are *you*?"

He didn't hesitate. "Four inches."

I thought he had to be kidding. Who brags about a four-inch cock? I wanted to laugh, not at his size but at his style, until I realized it would devastate him.

"And you?" he asked, now trying to be tough, his hands balled up on his hips.

"You'll see," I managed.

Needless to say, I stood him up. It wasn't a terribly deliberate choice. I was tired, I wasn't in the mood for the lake, and I thought he was kind of weird anyway. But a few days later, he found me in my favorite beach chair, reading. To my surprise, he casually settled on the sand next to me, crossing his legs as if to meditate.

"Hello," he said, a little embarrassed. "Have you got the sports section there?" He nodded at the *Tribune* folded on my lap.

"The Cubs lost," I said as I handed him the paper. I was expecting him to stretch out and start posing for me and everybody else, but he remained Buddha-like, turning the pages with a wet fingertip.

"I don't care about the Cubs," he said, his eyes on the newspaper. "I like football better."

I thought he meant soccer, so I didn't have much to say. "I don't keep up with sports," I told him. He seemed so different now, his face boyish and sweet. "What's the name of our team—The Sting, The Stingers—?"

He looked up at me, amused. "Not *futbol*," he said. "I mean American football. You know, the contact sport." He winked at me. I took note that his wife and kids were nowhere in sight.

❊   ❊   ❊

I can't really explain how it happened after that, other than to say that suddenly Rogelio was in my orbit. He is no less married, no less a parent—in fact, he is, above all, a family man—and how he manages to juggle it all has always amazed me. Part of it is simple: The man does not consider himself even vaguely homosexual. Instead, he thinks of himself as *sexual*, as capable of sex with a cantaloupe as with a woman or a man. It's a definition that deals in quantity and athleticism and has little, if any, relationship to love or pleasure.

For all of his sexual posturing, however, it was I who

taught *him* how to kiss—rather, that it's okay to kiss another man. Before, Rogelio could make love all day without puckering up even once. He is sure, because there are certain things he will not do in bed with a man, and because of—quite literally—his favorite sexual positions, that he's a man in the old fashioned sense of the word.

We hadn't been friends long when I got sick. It started simply enough—just a cough, a kind of constant fatigue. But Rogelio was astonishingly tender, stopping by with groceries, making thick Mexican bean soups, and actually tucking me in before leaving for the night shift on the South Side. He tried to be nonchalant about it. He said these were all parental skills and that my apartment was on the way to this or that errand.

I'd already concluded that he needed to have these self-delusions, so I didn't bother to point out that I was easily thirty minutes north of his family's home. There are plenty of hardware stores and laundromats in his neighborhood, so all his errands could have been run locally. And his little pit stop at my place meant it took more than an hour for him to get to his factory job. But, hey, I loved his attentions. And as it turned out, he was a fountain of unexpected kindnesses, one after another. It wasn't just the things he did. It was the *way* he did them. There was little mistaking his concern, or even—as strange as this may sound—his devotion. Against all odds, he's always believed I'll get better.

Most of my friends think Rogelio's cute, but pretty transient, too (he's living in the U.S. thanks to a rather dubious green card). We've taken him to a couple of gay bars, but he just stands around, giggling incessantly. He's too shy to dance and too scared to be comfortable. Once, we dragged him to a gay street fair, and even though there were plenty of straight people there—mostly whites—he did seem relaxed. I told him he looked great in the sunshine, with his dark brown skin and all, and a couple of the guys started ribbing me good-naturedly about being a Cha Cha Queen. Surprisingly, even Rogelio joined in.

But for all his involvement with me and his socializing with my friends in New Town, Rogelio always deals with gays as "other." Once, when my friend Stan was over, I put my arm around Rogelio's shoulder, and he violently shook it off. "I'm the man here," he told me. Stan snapped, "Honey, you know what they say...'The butchier the boy, the higher his legs go.'" At first I thought there might be blood on my walls, but Rogelio just giggled. That night, I put him out on the streets.

I've tried to talk to him about this, not out of any particular political conviction, but because I think there's an absurdity in pretending he's so hyper-masculine while he's scratching at my door. Personally, I think he knows better.

Later, I asked him if he understood what Stan had meant, and he made it quite clear that he did. He also said his toes rarely left the sheets. I said that wasn't true, but Rogelio thought the best way to prove his point was just to show me.

* * *

When my diagnosis came through, I surprised myself by not being devastated. I think I already knew. Three of my former lovers had already died of AIDS, and I've been around the block too many times not to be at risk. But when the social worker at the clinic urged me to tell my sexual partners and encourage them to go for counseling, I did have a moment of panic. How the hell would I tell Rogelio? Not telling him was out of the question—I never doubted the boy's sexual prowess; besides his wife, I was sure there were dozens of others, men and women.

For the record, I've never been around Rogelio without a parachute. In spite of all his efforts to the contrary, we've never engaged in anything but the safest sex. Still, there are so many things that can happen, so there was little question about my responsibility to tell him.

It wasn't easy. I took him out for a beer at a neighborhood bar and explained it as best I could: that I'd had an HIV test which had come back positive, that I'd had the Western blot, and it was positive, too. I told him I was symptomatic, that my swollen glands and fatigue were typical.

"Who gave it to you?" he asked me, his face blank from shock. We were sitting on a pair of stools at the bar, and the neon from behind the register cast an eerie green glow across his features. He looked monstrous, and for the first time since I'd known him, I wanted to get away from him.

"Don't you understand what I just said?"

"Yes, I understand," he said, looking down at his feet. "And I want to know who gave it to you, okay?" His palms rested on his thighs.

"Rogelio, who the fuck knows who gave it to me?"

"Well, you know, don't you?"

"No, I don't; how could I? It could be anybody. And it doesn't matter anyway."

"It doesn't matter?" he asked, amazed. His face contorted with anger. "I want to know who it is, so I can kill the son of a bitch."

"Look, Rogelio, my honor isn't what's at stake here," I said, tired of the school yard bully in him. "It's you—and your family. You've probably been exposed."

"But Tommy," he said, his eyes narrowing into slits. "I'm not going to get this sickness. You, yes—you're a homosexual."

I shrank from him, feeling my fingertips go cold. I wanted to go running down the street, not to believe we'd ever shared an intimate moment or any kind of peace together. This was a monster of a man, the cruel stranger who offered candy from the sedan window. I don't know how it happened, only that suddenly I had my fingers wrapped like rope around his neck. His face disappeared into the black beneath the bar as I screamed at him. It was an awful, primitive howl.

"You and your fucking masculinity!" I shouted, my hands going numb as I tried to strangle him. There were sudden, loud noises in the bar and stools toppling over, men hooking my arms with theirs and pulling, pushing. "You can marry Miss Mexico and have a million little Third World babies, and it won't keep your cock from going up every time you're with a man, motherfucker! I've seen you!"

Somebody else's arm tightened around my throat, pulling me off Rogelio, but I kept screaming and kicking, or trying to, until I was chest-down on the floor. Somebody sat on my shoulders, and somebody else held my hands behind my back. "Calm down, Tommy," said a familiar voice. "Just calm down, baby."

I turned my head enough to see Rogelio being picked up off the floor by a muscular black man who held him as if he were a toy. His face was red, and his nose ran bloody all over his shirt.

"You okay, Tommy?" said the voice on top of me, which I recognized as Stan's. I thought his weight would flatten my lungs. "If I let you up, Tom, are you going to be okay?"

I grunted something that meant yes, and he hopped off me, finally allowing me to breathe. Stan smoothed my hair with one hand and used the other to help me up, but I was dizzy and terrified I was going to pass out.

"Just hold onto me if you need to, Tommy," he said, being gentle and sweet. He kept the circle of men around us at a safe distance. The fight had drawn quite a crowd. I noticed Arthur, the bar owner, staring at me.

"I'm sorry," I mumbled, but Stan just shook his head, telling me it was all right. My knees felt slippery; I had no energy. Stan pushed me against a chair.

"How about a glass of water for Tommy?" he said in Arthur's direction, and one appeared almost instantly. Stan wiped my face with a napkin and smiled. "You almost killed him," he said.

I looked across the room to where Rogelio had buried his face in the black man's shoulder. At first I thought the bastard was necking with him, but then I realized from the way his body shook that he was sobbing, right there in front of everybody.

"You want to tell me about it?" Stan asked.

I sighed. I knew Arthur wouldn't ban me for starting the fight, but the only decent thing would be to leave and not come back for a few weeks. I looked around the room, where most of the other men were relaxing now, the danger having passed. Stan, my healthy, good-looking buddy, was rubbing my shoulders. I hugged him and kissed his ear.

"Come on," he said, pulling back a little. "Tell Auntie Stan."

I chuckled. He can be such a queen sometimes. "It was nothing," I said. "You know...AIDS-related dementia." Then I cried and cried.

* * *

Rogelio and I wound up speeding down Interstate 55 together for the same reason, I suppose, that desperate people do desperate things. As awful as it can be, there's a strange sense we're all we've got. Of course, I know that's not quite true, and he probably does, too. Right now Rogelio is quietly bitching about having to stop in St. Louis. He's in a hurry to get to Santa Fe only because it's our goal; of course, I'm in no hurry at all. The mountains will still be there, as will Ron and Paul, their leather boys and buffalo skulls.

"There's a sign for the Arch," I say, pointing.

"Okay, okay," Rogelio sighs, resigned to playing tourist. I can tell he thought we might pass it without my noticing. "I see it." He means the Arch itself, which is shimmering just off the highway. Frankly, the Arch is the only thing I've ever noticed about St. Louis—that silver loop rising out of the riverfront. Otherwise, St. Louis seems pretty flat and innocuous; it could be any one of a million cities.

"Do you know anything about the Arch?" I ask Rogelio, but he just shakes his head. "I wonder what kind of view it has." Then I realize I'm not really thinking of St. Louis, but of Chicago, which is breathtaking from both the Sears Tower and the John Hancock. The panorama is more industrial, more metropolitan and complete from Sears, but I prefer the Hancock, with its strapping steel embrace. From the Hancock's east windows the lake is an endless sheen of blue. As I picture it—the lake dotted with tiny sailboats and specks of people on the shore—I realize I'll never see my hometown again. "Is the Arch a memorial or something?" I ask.

"I don't know, I don't have any idea," Rogelio says as he turns off the interstate and onto a busy city street. He's annoyed.

"Hmmm, does St. Louis have much of a skyline?" I'm determined to ignore his mood.

"I don't think so," Rogelio says. We're now stopped at a light, and the Arch is just to our right. The top of it disappears into the sky. "I don't think St. Louis has much of anything."

"Well, it's got Busch Stadium," I tell him.

"So what?" he says. "St. Louis lost the Cardinals to Phoenix."

"The football team, yeah, but not the baseball team."

We ride alongside the Mississippi River, where the city fathers are trying to develop a mall of sorts. There are a couple of riverboats that look permanently moored and have trendy hand-painted signs advertising authentic river cuisine, whatever that is. Rogelio grunts. He tries to figure out where to park, wanting to avoid the lots nestled under the interstate. We haven't seen a cop anywhere, our car is filled with my things, and Rogelio's silently convinced that leaving the car in the unguarded lot will spell trouble.

"You're the only Latin I know who doesn't care about baseball," I say. We take another turn, and I shade my eyes as I look at the glistening river. I need to buy sunglasses; I'll certainly use them in Santa Fe.

"I think Americans make too much of Latin fascination with baseball," he says, trying to relax.

"There are plenty of Latins at Cubs games," I say.

"Ah, yes, but that has another purpose," Rogelio says, finally emitting a little laugh. "That has to do with psychological identification." He's loose enough now to consider the parking lot, which is empty of all human life.

"Oh really?"

He smiles. "People call the Cubs 'lovable losers,' right?" he asks, while pulling a ticket from the machine at the lot's entrance. He maneuvers the car around the gravel and next to the chain-link fence. We are in the most exposed space in the lot.

"So?"

"Well, it fits in perfectly with the Latin inferiority complex," he explains with a cynical smile. "We're just trying to figure out why people like them, so we can imitate them." He turns off the car, pops his seat belt, and is out before I have a chance to hug him, which I very much want to do.

■   ■   ■

The Arch is just beyond us, on the other side of a well-manicured little park. It looks a lot like the McDonald's arch, only big and made of chrome. When I try to look at it, the reflection is blinding. "God, it's bright," I say. I'm dizzy again.

"Do you want me to help you?" Rogelio's standing above me, watching as I try to get out of the car.

I shake my head. "It'll pass. I just need a minute."

"No problem," he says, but his foot is twitching, almost tapping. The muscles in his arms are tight again.

"You look just like you did that first day," I say, but actually he looks better.

"So do you," he lies, and reaches over to ruffle my hair. His touch is a little rough, but it's kind.

Of course, I look nothing like I did then. I'm pale and wasted, and I know my eyes are sinking into darkness. I wait a few minutes, then push myself off the car seat. I hold the car door for balance and notice Rogelio's worried but impatient look.

"Are you sure you want to do this?" he asks. I nod. "They probably have one of those elevators like at the Sears Tower—you leave your stomach on the ground level. It might make you sick."

I smile at him. "I think I can handle it. Besides, if I get dizzy again, I'll hold on to you." I wink.

"Uh uh," he says, shaking his head, but he's still smiling. "What you need is to get to Santa Fe and relax with your friends."

"Rogelio, I'm not going to get better," I tell him as we step onto the picturesque walkway to the Arch.

"Sure you are."

"Only for a little while," I say, measuring my breath as we walk up the hill. Then I casually reach over to him and touch his fingers. He looks around quickly and obviously, but he doesn't freak out or push me away, as I might have expected. Instead, his hand covers and squeezes mine. I'm just thinking how exhilarating—and amazing—this is, when we hear a voice behind us.

"Excuse me."

Rogelio stiffens, then moves his hand to my elbow as he turns toward me, pretending he's helping me walk. His eyes are panic-stricken and silently pleading with me to cooperate with his charade.

"Excuse me," the voice says again, and Rogelio whirls around, momentarily stumped when he can't find the source. When his eyes finally focus down on two women in wheelchairs trying to get by us, he jumps dramatically out of the way, muttering excuses under his breath.

"My god," he says, panting. "Where did they come from?"

"I think they're racing," I say as the two shiny chairs disappear over the hill.

"Do you think they saw?" he asks.

"Saw what?" I'm disgusted: it wasn't the women who ruined the moment, it was him. He doesn't understand, but he feels badly and tries to make light of the situation by throwing his hands in the air in mock resignation. The problem is, I'm too angry, too disappointed to think it's even a little amusing.

"We don't have a lot of time," I tell him, gasping on the incline.

"Then let's hurry," he says, checking his watch and quickening his step toward the Arch. But he's misunderstood me again.

■ ■ ■

The fact is, I don't really want to deal with the Arch, and I don't really want to go to Santa Fe, which rings in my ears with an unexpected finality. About the only place I want to be is on the front porch of Stan's old house, just a couple of blocks off Broadway back in Chicago. I spent the whole summer of 1978 lounging on that porch, reading about Anita Bryant's antigay crusade in the papers and watching the boys walk by.

I fell in love a million times that season, and each time there would be a triumphant moment when my new lover and I would walk hand in hand down Broadway. I had a real swagger then; I wore satin running shorts and sunglasses at night. At least half the fun came from the stares we got from the Greek restaurant owners and Korean dry cleaners. Gay men were all over Broadway then, even more so than now— we were the guys ordering gyros and bringing in Italian suits to be pressed, so nobody complained. We always said we didn't care what people thought, but we did. And back then we cared even more. Public displays of affection were a statement: No queers had done it before, not like that—right there at high noon, trying desperately to make it seem as commonplace as taking a baby for a stroll.

"Are you okay?" Rogelio asks as we near the Arch. My breathing is labored and my chest feels tight.

I can tell he's afraid I'll get morbid on him; he practically cringes in anticipation. I do want to tell him the truth, but I don't have the energy. As soon as I can, I sit down on the concrete steps just below the Arch, fold my arms on my knees, and put my head down. My legs seem extraordinarily long, and my head feels like a drum.

"Are you all right?" asks a stranger's voice.

I look up enough to make out one of the wheelchair women. "I'm okay," I tell her; she seems totally trustworthy. "I'm just a little dizzy." Her friend is waiting for her, parked about ten yards from us but facing the parking lot. "You already went up?" I ask, surprised that they're ready to leave so soon.

"We can't go up," she says, and her tone is both wry and resigned. "The Arch isn't accessible."

I can tell Rogelio doesn't understand, his eyes scanning mine for meaning. "There aren't any ramps?" I ask the woman, thinking Rogelio and I can help them, but then I realize I'm too weak to push a wheelchair, much less lift one, or two.

She laughs, but it isn't bitter or mean. "Not just that," she says. "The elevators aren't accessible either." Now I'm as confused as Rogelio, but before I have a chance to ask her anything, she's saying good-bye and rolling back to her friend.

※　※　※

There's a whole subterranean world under the Arch: a museum, a video show, a couple of souvenir stores. There's also a snake of a line to the elevators. I'm surprised there are so many people, especially because it's a weekday, but then I realize most of the ticket holders are tourists, primarily Asians. Even though the line moves relatively well, I have to squat and lean against the wall. It's getting harder to swallow, too, and I keep seeing little bursts of orange and blue light in front of my eyes.

During all this, Rogelio is a phantom. He stands pale and quiet next to me, but he wants to run. His fingers are folded into tentative fists, and he keeps shifting his eyes from side to side. I know the crowd scares him; there are too many people in uniform. I tell him these are only Arch security people, not covert INS agents. But although he has never gotten so much as a traffic ticket, authority types frighten him, and he won't be reassured.

Me, I resent everything. I hate that with a mouthful of thrush I'm the one having to tell him everything's okay. For once, I want him to do the talking, I want him to be brave, to take my hand, push his way to the front of the line and demand our own elevator. At the top of the Arch, I want us to grope and run our tongues along each other's stubbly chins, right there in front of all the tourist groups and grade-school field trips.

"Tommy?" There's a hand on my cheek. "Tommy?" I lift my eyes and see Rogelio's face emerging from a gray haze. "We should go," he says. "You don't look good." He glances nervously next to me, where a woman with two small children is staring at us.

"Fuck what I look like," I say, my lips sticking to each other. I reach up to undo my mouth, but I can barely feel my fingers.

"Tommy, let's go," Rogelio insists, and he starts to take my elbow.

"No, damn it," I say, standing up and jerking away. "I don't want to go to Santa Fe yet." I think of those ghostly buffalo skulls hung so artfully in Ron and Paul's gallery. "I have a fashionable disease, you know." Rogelio blanches, and I laugh. "Hey, don't worry, you're not going to get it," I add, winking at him. I start to laugh again, but something gets caught in my throat, and I cough instead, my head rocking back and forth. After a minute, I see him through the watery channel in my eyes. He has stepped away a bit, almost as if he's scared of me.

"You look like shit," he says in a whisper.

Soon we're in front of the elevators, and I understand why the wheelchair women were disenfranchised: You have to step up and hunch down to get in the elevators, which aren't elevators at all but tiny little holding pens in which no one can stand. The doors open and shut like a vault. As I watch the tourists get in, I can't help but think of Nazi ovens. A few people refuse to ride these little torture chambers, and I think they look suspiciously Jewish.

"Get in, Tommy," Rogelio orders, and I lift my legs one at a time, but I fall anyway, finally crawling up to a chair. I want to tell Rogelio I don't think we'll survive, but the only thing out of my mouth is air. I finally settle in, wiping my face on my sleeve, which is so wet I could wring it. I feel bruised and weary.

Rogelio says nothing, he just sits quietly across from the two Asians assigned with us to this elevator. They are blank-faced and embarrassed. I supply the soundtrack for the trip, breathing like an iron lung. When the elevator starts moving—not a modern vacuum up some gigantic shaft but a jerky Ferris wheel ride—they're relieved to hear the creaking and groaning of the gears.

I look out the little window and realize we have no view at all. Instead, we're traversing the very bowels of the St. Louis Arch—ancient stairwells, a landing filled with janitorial supplies, a caged room with lockers for maintenance workers. I start to laugh, quietly at first, but then I can't help it, and I slap my thigh hysterically.

Rogelio ignores me at first, then finally reaches over and reluctantly pats my shoulder. "Don't cry, Tommy," he says. But I'm not crying at all. I wipe my nose and brush my hair out of my face. I pull my pants up and dry my eyes. Then I tuck in my shirt, feeling the vast distance between my bones and the waistband.

"I don't ever want to get to Santa Fe," I say after much effort, and Rogelio shakes his head. He can't hear me above the mechanical noises. The Asians across from us shift in their seats, and Rogelio sits as far away from me as space allows. "I don't want to go to Santa Fe," I repeat, but I can't feel my lips move.

※　※　※

When the elevator doors part, we tumble out to a steep, narrow stairway. We're all crushed together, the Asians,

Rogelio, and me, and traffic keeps going around us. I feel Rogelio's hands on my hips, secretly guiding me up toward the fresh-faced student at the top of the stairs, a red-haired girl with a walkie-talkie strapped to her belt. She's on the lookout for trouble, or troublemakers, and it feels like Rogelio's turning me in. I jerk him loose, pushing my way through the crowd. It's cold up here, and the air feels thin.

At the top, the observation deck is a small room that resembles a space capsule. There are no windows to speak of, just horizontal slits maybe a yard wide and ten inches deep. To get a peek you lean over, resting your body against the incline of the walls. On the east side, there's no lake, just the Mississippi River looking muddy and small. On the west, there's no city, just generic St. Louis. Straight down, I can see the kidney-shaped pond next to the Arch and the walkway to the parking lot. I'm nauseous.

"Rogelio?" I whisper. I don't see him anywhere. A couple of kids are running between adult legs, but none belong to Rogelio. I try to find him by stretching up above the crowd, but I can't seem to muster the strength. I lean my back against the wall and feel my throat with my hand. My fingers seem to be working again, and my glands aren't as tender. I lick my lips, but there's something salty on them. I turn away from the crowd, which keeps brushing against me, and flap my sleeve up to my mouth. My lips feel sore.

It's then I hear unmistakable laughter behind me: high-pitched, kind of girlish. I turn to find it, but whole family groups keep coming and going by me as quickly and enthusiastically as if we were at a political rally. Everybody's got souvenir tee-shirts. There's a grandmother with a Confederate flag sewn on the back of her jacket. Teenage girls cackle with disappointment over the Arch's antiquated futurism. They smack their gum and sigh, barely noticing me. They're so close, I can smell their shampoo and cigarettes.

"St. Louis used to have another baseball team, before the Cardinals," someone is saying; it's a voice I could recognize in the dark. "But the St. Louis Browns left the city and became the Baltimore Orioles in 1954." There's a man with a cowboy hat in front of me, and as the hat dances away, I see Rogelio, cocky, giving away no secrets. He's talking to another man, propped casually against the wall on the other side.

"Well, it's karma then," the man says. He's big and white and wearing a cap with the logo from Rogelio's union local. "You know, Baltimore had a team sneak out on 'em a couple of years ago—the Colts."

"Yes, the football team," Rogelio says. "They're in Indianapolis now."

The man, who's about fifty and graying, hunches forward to look out one of the little windows. I can't keep them in my line of vision because the tourist flow is constant. But I hear them both laugh. Then I see the man slap Rogelio's shoulder in a friendly, manly sort of way. They're obviously friends, and when a small woman in a pair of yellow cotton pants comes up to them, the man goes through a series of introductory motions. Rogelio shakes her hand.

I'm watching from across the way, but he has no idea I'm here. So many people have bumped into me, I feel raw and beaten. I want to leave now; I want to collect my lover and go. "Rogelio," I say, but he doesn't hear me. A girl walking inches in front of me focuses my way. She's not sure if I'm talking to her. "I'm just trying to get my boyfriend's attention," I tell her, nodding in Rogelio's direction. The girl looks frightened, and I feel something wet on my shirt. Someone says something to her over her shoulder, but her eyes are wary and still on me.

I try to get away, but my knees wobble, and I quickly lean back against the wall. I touch my uneasy stomach, rubbing it with my hand. When I reach up to my pounding heart, I find a puddle and follow the trail of saliva up to my chin. I shove my wrist up to my mouth, rubbing my sleeve against it. I turn around slowly, facing the wall, and swallow hard. My forehead throbs. I tell myself it's not a good idea to panic. I remind myself the St. Louis Arch is not accessible, and I'm going to have to walk back to one of those little Nazi elevators. But I don't want to move, I don't want anything to happen now. I want to close my eyes and open them up to the aftermath of a simple dizzy spell in a normal world, where Rogelio comes up from behind me while I'm doing the dishes and wraps me up, nuzzling against my neck.

"Mister, are you all right?"

The red-haired girl with the walkie-talkie is standing next to me. She is all business, and her look is firm. I'd tell her I'm fine, but I'm not. And besides, I could never fool her.

"Do you need help?" she asks, and it's obvious I do. "Here," she says, offering her shoulder as a crutch. She uses a free hand to unhook the walkie-talkie from her belt and gives emergency instructions across the air waves. Then she efficiently snaps it back on her belt and turns to me, holding me with strong, muscular arms. I push slowly off the wall and turn.

The entire observation deck is quiet now, and the crowd has created a space for me. The only sounds are the elevators in the distance and the shuffling of feet. The red-haired girl walks with me, and I hear whispers behind me. As we head toward the stairway, the noise level returns to normal. I hear Rogelio's voice again, and my head jerks toward it. The red-haired girl turns with me.

"Rogelio—"

His back is to us, and he stabs the air with his finger to make a point in an argument. The gray-haired man with whom he's talking sees us and juts his chin our way. Rogelio turns quickly, registering everything with a shiver. Suddenly, he looks just like any other South Side greaser—the too-tight blue jeans and black tee-shirt, his hands rough and calloused. His chest moves up and down with heavy breathing.

My eyelids drop against my will, and the red-haired girl shifts under me. I hear her say something, and Rogelio responds, but when I finally look up all I see is his shoulder turning back to the gray-haired man and the woman in the yellow pants, their voices unnaturally bright. I hear him say something about his son, about football, about his wife. I don't know, I don't know.

I want to throw up. Both Rogelio and I have keys to the car, but I know neither one of us would leave the other. The thing is, I've seen him turn now, and I've heard his voice bob and sink away from me. That means something.

When the red-haired girl leads me away, I look over her shoulder, wanting by sheer force, by the volume of both my love and hatred, to make Rogelio look at me. When he finally does, just this side of the heterosexual couple pretending not to notice our intensity, he's terrified. He sticks his hands in his jeans pockets and balls them up, causing the jeans themselves to hike up an inch or so. He looks at me, then looks away. Then he looks back again, his eyes pleading for understanding. But my heart is pounding its thin walls, and I don't understand. I want to ask him how much he expects me to take.

Special thanks to Gabor and Rex Wockner.

Man Oh Man

an oh man, Ice is dead, as cold and white as shrimp.
I'm telling you this because I want it to make
sense, you know? I want you to understand that I
knew nothing about it, other than that I was there, or rather,
here, and that at one point I noticed the stuff that I thought
was just beer on the floor was his blood, still gooey, still red
in the middle and black around the edges of each puddle. I
was sitting right in the big one, right in the one where he
died, the one that killed him. It ruined my jacket, the one
with all the zippers and patches. It'll never come off, not
really, not ever.

Man oh man, it's tough to believe because just last night
Ice was standing in the middle of my kitchen, flapping his
arms around like a bird, talking about spring, talking about
going to Florida or California or maybe New York City. He
was saying we could have a kid, such a pretty kid, and smart,
too, and *wise*, like us.

Ice, I said, man oh man, you're crazy, and he laughed and
laughed, and then I laughed, too. That's all you can do sometimes, you know, laugh. And since we found out from the
public health clinic, when we called up and got our little
anonymous numbers checked, and the nurse on the phone
wouldn't tell either one us if we were positive or negative but
wanted us to come in and be counseled—counseled, can you
imagine *that?*—well, we just *knew*, and so we'd been laughing
lately even more than usual.

We were still laughing when we got in his car and drove
over here, where Luís had promised us some stuff. Luís owed
it to us. We'd helped him last month, not just about dope but

with a coat, 'cause it was still really cold then. It's hard to get a coat for a guy Luís's size. I don't know where Ice got it—it fit perfect even though Luís is big and scaly like a dinosaur—and Ice kept teasing him that he'd had it tailor-made. Funny, huh?

You know, Ice was in a really good mood last night, like if he'd had anything, he would have definitely given it away by the end of the night. You know what I mean?

Well, we got here and Luís had the lights off and a bunch of candles lit. He introduced us to a girl named Daisy, whose face looked all punched in, not from fists or anything like that, but just as if she were born that way—punched in, squashed. Her hair was real long and fine and didn't fit with the rest of her. I thought it might be a wig, except that there wasn't much of it, and you could see the roots coming out of her scalp. Luís seemed proud of her one minute, then disgusted the next, like he just couldn't make up his mind.

She did what he said, though, like putting all the stuff right in front of Ice, like he was the high priest or something. You know, I can do it better than Ice, except when there's other people around, he just *has to* do it—it's his trip, his macho thing. I fought with him about it a couple of times, but after the call to the clinic it just seemed silly. Who cares, really? Let's just get on with it, that's what I say.

Ice set the spoon on Luís's coffee table, the one that looks like a wagon wheel, and pressed his thumb on the handle to hold it down tight. You wouldn't think a spoon could move on its own, but sometimes, I swear, they get electric or some-thing. Then he held one of the little bags up between the thumb and index finger of his other hand and tapped some of the powder with the back of his middle finger.

He's real slow, you know. He likes to take his time, to watch every little movement. He says it's a sacrament. I've never seen him even a little desperate. Sometimes I catch a little bit of sweat glistening there under his moustache, but that's it, that's the closest he gets to nervous. Luís likes to watch him, too, like Ice's an artist or a great chef. Daisy, on the other hand, she was bitchy. It's not that she said anything, but she kept smoking cigarettes, pulling them from her squashed-in face with jerky little movements, then sucking them up again.

But Ice was cool, telling stories, humming while he watched the drop of water fall from his fingertip to the top of the white powder in the spoon, then lifting the spoon up like it was holy wine and lighting his Graceland lighter under it.

He really bought that damn thing at Graceland, in Memphis, when he and Luís went one day just because they were on the interstate with a full tank of gas and enough money to get there and back. You didn't want me to die without ever having been to Graceland, did you? he asked when he got back, grinning and exhausted, wet and shaking. And I said, well, what about me, huh?

But he never answered, just talked about the Jungle Room and how Elvis's middle name is misspelled on his tombstone. Make sure my name is spelled right, he said. If they can do that to Elvis, man oh man, they can do that to me. And I told him I wanted to be cremated, so nobody ever had to worry about me again, and besides, it seemed fitting to become dust. I asked Ice if you could smoke ashes or melt them and shoot them up, but he just got angry, really, really angry, so I let it go. I don't like fighting with him.

Well, after we were all ready, after Ice had pulled his needle from his boot and had the plunger in and was ready to load, Daisy says, No. She says she's not using his needle. He asked her if she'd fucked Luís yet, and she told him it was none of his goddamn business.

Well, Ice just looks over at Luís, who's baring his little

yellow prehistoric teeth. But Ice didn't care. You didn't tell her, man? he asks. And Luís nods and shrugs and says, Yeah, but they're *practicing safe sex*. Well, that's cool, Ice tells him, except we're all going to die anyway. And then he puts the needle in the stuff, fills it up good, squirts the bubbles out, and says, Who's first?

When nobody volunteered, I volunteered. Besides being a natural ice-breaker (ha ha), I was starting to need it, too. I was getting cold. So Ice says, Okay, and he gives me the needle and comes over and holds my arm.

We don't tie off because, well, you don't really need to anyway, but Ice thinks it's kind of sick, like S/M or something, and he prefers to just squeeze my arm. It's a connection we make, something like sex, only warmer.

Actually, I don't need his help. And he doesn't need mine either, although I squeeze his arm, too. We've both got blue thumb marks around our biceps from all that gripping. But the fact is, all four of our arms—do we sound like an octopus?—are thin enough where they need to be, and our veins are out there enough that all we really need to do is point, shoot, and fold up.

Then Ice turned to Daisy and said, You're next. She nodded, but instead of putting her arm out she turns to Luís and asks him something in Spanish, and he nods his head yes.

I was starting to warm up by then. I was starting to feel the syrup-thing—that's what we call it—when you feel your feet like they're an Aunt Jemima bottle filling up with maple syrup, only it's hot and sugary, and you can smell it, too— that is, you can feel it inside you, like at knee-level, and smell it at the same time. Does that make sense? Anyway, that's where I was at.

The next thing I know, Daisy's got a metal salad bowl full of cloudy white bleach, and she's ripping a package of Handi-

Wipes open with her teeth. She's really struggling, you know, tugging on the damn plastic wrapping until it finally stretches too far, and she pokes a finger into a little hole in the stretch and just rips it open with one big jerk. Man oh man, I felt sorry for her.

Ice handed her the needle, and she put it in the bowl, filled it up and emptied it a bunch of times, and then, finally, she said she was ready. Ice was trying not to laugh, I could tell. The whole time she's talking about how a social worker from the University of Illinois taught her that. Luís just kept looking at her, one minute fascinated, the next minute repulsed. I didn't blame him, not really.

Then she tied off, as you might expect, and Luís did it for her. What surprised me was that then she started doing all that washing again for Luís like it would make a difference after all the times he's been with us, or like he couldn't do it for himself. The thing is, the stuff hit her pretty hard and pretty fast. You could tell: her hands looked like little balls of uncooked dough, threatening to crumble and fall apart. And Ice, who doesn't believe in the bleach, was getting impatient with her.

Didn't you ever work as a busboy? he asked Luís, who didn't say anything as he rolled up his sleeve. Dishwasher? Ice asked. Hey, are those rubbers in your pocket, man? Ice kept teasing him. What about you, Daisy? Ever been a masseuse? A switchboard operator?

The way Daisy was working in that bowl, you'd think she was doing the laundry for a whole Indian tribe. I kept waiting for her to hit the needle against the bowl like it was dirty clothes getting knocked on a rock at a riverside, and to scrub, scrub, scrub, then hang that syringe out to dry before letting the guys use it. Ice sighed one of his long sighs and dropped back on the couch.

Hell, I was pretty much syrup by then, just dripping down

there to the floor. I remember getting there and putting my head down. I could smell Luís's dirty old dog on the rug, all mildewy and black. I don't know where the dog was, or where it went to, or even what kind of dog it is. I couldn't tell you that stuff, only that it was shaggy. And that it left its smell on the rug. Can you still smell it, or has Ice's blood overpowered it? It'd have to be strong blood, but I guess he had that, no matter what those folks at the clinic said.

I woke up just a couple of hours ago, I guess. I looked up, and there was that wooden beam on Luís's ceiling. I do remember Luís and Ice arguing, their voices going up and bumping against that beam, but I don't know what they were talking about. I really don't. I was one warm, gooey puddle by then.

All I know is I woke up with my head on Ice's stomach. He felt flabby, you know, like all his muscle had been loosened up. His back was leaning up against Luís's couch. I felt around, and everything was sticky on the floor and on my jacket and jeans. I remember I heard music and stuff, and I kept thinking maybe I'd been out of it, and we'd had a party or something. I didn't know. Who knows these things?

I thought Ice was still passed out, so I got up real slow. I saw what looked like a refrigerator light coming from the other room, but it turned out to be a night light in the bathroom—in the shape of a cow, no less. I found this out when I got to the bathroom and decided to wash my face, to freshen up, maybe take a bath. The little cow light was all aglow. I didn't really want to wash up, but it's like when I was doing LSD. See, I knew I had to eat after crashing, or I'd have stomach pains all the next day from the speed, so I made myself eat whether I was hungry or not. Since I do junk—I'm no fool, you know, I had junkie friends before, and I knew they stunk—I make myself get clean. I mean, I nearly drown sometimes, but I'll be damned if

I'm going to be avoided on the subway. You know what I mean?

Well, I'm scrubbing off the soap into a sink full of pinkish water when I look up and see myself in the mirror that's the medicine cabinet, and I think, shit, I look like Daisy. I mean, suddenly my face is all caved in, too; my cheeks are concave, my bones, everything. I get all the soap off and rip a towel off the rack and rub, and I'm still all punched in, even my mouth is.

This is pretty scary business, you know, and I go, Ice, Ice, man oh man, come here, I'm all squash-faced like Daisy. But he doesn't hear me, so I yell again, Ice, man, c'mere. But nothing. In fact, I think I'm the only person left in the house, like not only are Luís and Daisy gone, but maybe Ice got up and left, too, while I was washing my face. And I get *really* scared, my heart beating faster and faster.

I run out of there. I run like crazy into the living room, I almost trip over a little throw rug in the hallway that tries to slide out from under me, and I make it to Ice, who's still all sprawled out on the floor, his head leaning back on the couch. All I can see is the right side of his face. Ice, I say, Ice, man oh man, wake up.

I tug on his shirt a little, then I turn his face around, to shake him, so when he opens his eyes he's staring right at me, and that's when I saw. I didn't have much choice because when I turned his head there was this exhausted sound like air being let out of a tire, and then that squishing sound, and something very red, and that completely new rush of blood followed by the flop-flop of stuff just dropping from his opened throat. I don't know what it was. It could have been food, except we hadn't eaten, or brains, or whatever. It looked like pieces of tampons.

So you see, I was there, or here, right here in the living room when it happened—whatever it is that happened. I probably saw the whole thing—but who knows what I saw? It could have been Daisy or Luís, or somebody entirely different. Maybe it was you or even me. Except I don't think it was me. Hell, I *know* it wasn't me. I was as good as Aunt Jemima then, and I...well, fuck, what difference does it make?

You're not going to believe me anyway, are you?

The Spouse

I was exactly noon, and the last of the weekend breakfast crowd filtered out of the diner. From the booth-lined back wall, a young woman made her way to the front to pay her check. She was tall, with reddish brown hair to her shoulders. When she stopped at the counter and fished through her shoulder bag for money, her tongue peeked out from between her teeth. She had a tattoo on her left wrist, a delicately etched silver and green double-headed ax. All around her the busboys and waitresses kept moving, the dishes clattering on the large trays. The register rang after each customer.

"Lupe!" a voice called from behind her.

She turned around, then frowned. Standing next to her was a dark, stocky young man, a few black hairs poking sharply out of his chin. He smiled sheepishly. He had on a stained white shirt and carried a tray of improbably balanced plates and glasses.

"Hello, Raul," she said, resigned to his recognition. "I didn't realize you worked here."

"Yes," he said, his English too formal, crackling with Spanish underneath. He glanced at the ax on her wrist. "Pedro got a job here, then he brought me. I've been here a few months already, so I should be a waiter soon."

Lupe pushed her check at the woman behind the register, then grunted and nodded at Raul.

"My English is much better now, don't you think?" he asked, watching as she dropped her change into the shoulder bag. The dishes on the tray rattled as he struggled to keep them from crashing to the floor.

"Yes," she said, starting out the door of the diner.

Raul hurried to get rid of the tray and followed her out through the vestibule to the sidewalk. The sudden sunlight was so intense that she was temporarily blinded, and she stopped, then pulled on her sunglasses. Her lenses framed his image: a small man but strong, his shoulders and arms thick with muscle.

"I haven't seen you in a long time," he said, now in Spanish. She noticed him studying her hands and made a fist, which caused the ax to expand.

"I haven't seen you since, well, you know. You said some very cruel things," he continued. "But I always look for you anyway, out in the streets, wondering how you are. You could have called."

"What for?"

Just then a pair of young men walked around them, one carrying a sheaf of flyers, the other a roll of tape and a stapler. They stopped and put up some of the papers on the telephone pole next to them, the stapler clicking over and over again. The two men, young and girlish, left after they'd layered the pole with announcements about an upcoming dance contest at a local club. Lupe lowered her glasses enough to read and register the information. Raul watched her.

"Well, you could call sometimes just to call, not for anything in particular, but to let me know how you are. I worry about you," he said.

"I'm sorry I didn't call," Lupe said. She pushed the black, impenetrable glasses back up her nose.

Raul grinned, suddenly absurdly happy at being with her. "You know, you could come by," he said.

"To do what?" Lupe sighed. "It would just get everybody worked up, or hopeful. It wouldn't be fair. I'd either have to deal with your family's judgments or lie about everything. It'd be horrible—and it'd just be for your ego, so you could be pitied or—" she chuckled, "admired."

"That's not true," Raul said, pouting. "It's just that...I mean, we're married, after all."

Lupe laughed. "No, Raul, *you're* married," she said. "You knew damn well this was just a convenience for me, a business deal. I can't help it that you've spun all these stories for your family." The sun was so bright she could barely see him. He was standing in front of the light, so his whole figure was one black block.

"But it's not right," Raul said. "I thought we would live together."

"I never agreed to that. If it had been a condition, I never would have married you." She was squinting; her mouth was dry.

He kicked around at a flyer that had come loose from the pole and wrapped itself around his trousers leg. He shook it off, then watched it fly down the street. "Well, I know I'm dependent on you, on your generosity on this matter—"

"No," she said, slashing her hand through the air. He watched the ax as if she were actually wielding it, and cringed.

"It's not generosity," Lupe said. "You paid me for something; all I'm doing is keeping my end of the bargain. And that doesn't include hanging around with you, your friends, or your family."

"Well, I think you need me, too," he said, his lower lip jutting out like a fleshy ledge. "I'm a good man; I can help you."

"You don't get it, Raul," Lupe said, shifting her weight from one hip to the other. She stood at an angle, scratched her hand. "I don't know that you'll ever get it, but suffice it to say that I don't need you. You can think I'm crazy—I don't care. We're not family, no matter how many justices of the peace we stand in front of."

"But of course we are!"

"No, Raul; you have your people and I have mine."

"But yours—that's not your family. You need me to help you stay in touch with your family, with your Latin self," he said angrily. He shoved one hand in his pants pocket and used the other to poke at the air. "In Mexico, this wouldn't happen, and you'd have to do as I say. There are laws, you know."

Lupe laughed again. "In Mexico, we'd never have married, Raul. In Mexico, you wouldn't *need* to marry a nice American girl."

"That's not what I married here. Besides, that you're American is an accident of geography," he said. "You're as Mexican as I am."

"Well, hell, Raul, if I'm as Mexican as you, then why do I need you to stay in touch with my Latin self?" she asked, mocking him.

"You're running away from your Latin self," he insisted. "You need me to remind you about who you *really* are. You need me to remember all your real feelings, to remember passion, and maybe think about motherhood and about music, and poetry, too."

"Raul, are you crazy?" Lupe asked incredulously. "Jesus, listen to that pile of stereotypes you just spit out. Passion? Poetry? And what in heaven's name makes you think I need you—of all people—to think about motherhood? Why would I need a man I hardly know to think about motherhood? You're a prick, Raul, a real prick."

"I know who you are," he went on. "And I know who you *think* you are. I'm a man who's seen a little bit of the world. I may not have gone to college like you, but I know people, and I know *you*."

"Look, Raul, you don't know me. We're married in name only; don't try to make more out of it," she said, exasperated. "Cut this shit out, okay? And please, quit looking for me on the streets, quit following me out of restaurants."

"Are you ashamed; is that it?"

"Of what?"

"Of what you're doing?"

"Oh, please," she said, and started to walk away. He shook his head sadly and looked down at the tips of his grime-covered shoes. Then he took off, following a few steps behind her.

"I didn't want to do this." he said, "But you've given me no choice." He tried to kick at a piece of concrete that stuck out from the sidewalk but missed, his leg swinging in the air.

"You're nuts, you know; you're absolutely nuts," she said, still walking, unaware of his bad aim.

Suddenly, he grabbed her and threw her against a flyer-covered telephone pole. "What the fuck do you think you're doing?" she demanded, kicking and scratching at him. Raul lowered his head to avoid her nails, but he continued holding her so tight that blue circles began forming on her skin under his fingers.

"I didn't want to hurt you," he said in a voice that cracked. "I tried to carry this around with me all by myself, but now you give me no choice." He yanked her up, pressing his body to hers and forcing her face to face with him. She could see his pores. He held her like that for a moment. Then, seeing the men with the flyers across the street, he let go, slowly dropping his hands to his sides but keeping his body so close that she couldn't escape. His face was pale and wet.

"Hit me and I'll kill you, motherfucker." Lupe tried to step away, readying her hands, martial arts style, for him. The ax on her wrist seemed to disappear in the light.

"You think I would hit you?" He closed his eyes, shook his head. "I am a *good* man, Lupe, don't you understand? No matter how mad I get, no matter how many times I may grab you, I'll never *hit* you."

"One more step toward me, Raul, and I'll have you

chopped like *picadillo*, baby." She swung her bag around her shoulder so it rested against her back. "Hey," she yelled in English to the two men across the street. "This guy's trying to kill me. Can you call the cops?" The two looked at each other warily then back across the street to Lupe in her battle stance.

Raul was crying. "The things you accuse me of, they're all the things that you do," he said, wiping his eyes with the back of his fists. "Well, I finally went and did one of them. It hurt me to do it, but I'm a man—I couldn't put up with this any longer."

"Hey, leave her alone," one of the men yelled from across the street, but it was lackluster. The second man walked slowly back to the diner where a blue metal flag advertised a public telephone inside.

"Raul, I don't want you near me, do you understand?" Lupe said, switching back to Spanish. "I don't know what the fuck you're talking about, but I'll tell you this much: if you keep this up, I'll file a police report, and the government will figure out what we're doing, and you will be shipped back. Do you understand?"

He didn't react to what she said. Instead, he took a deep breath and looked up at the sky. "I did it, you know," he finally said.

"Did what?" she asked, confused.

"I cheated on you," he said.

She stared at him. Her fighting posture loosened as she struggled for comprehension.

"I was with another woman," he said. "Since you wouldn't act like a wife, I just couldn't take it anymore, and I had an affair behind your back."

Lupe wanted to laugh but didn't. She was stunned by the hopeless sincerity of his unnecessary confession. "I think that's good, Raul," she finally said. "I think it's good that you get out and get involved. After all, we're not *really* married;

we're only *legally* married." She smiled a little as she talked, trying desperately to be supportive.

Raul closed his eyes, tears escaping from under the lids. "Oh, you are a cold, cold woman," he cried, his voice cracking again as he threw his hands in the air. "Why did I have to marry such a cold woman?"

"Raul, you didn't marry a cold woman; you married a lesbian."

He covered his ears with the palms of his hands. "I don't want to hear that," he shouted. "No! No! No!"

Lupe sighed and shook her head. "God, this is absolutely not worth it," she said, more to herself than to him.

"The cops are on their way," said the man who'd gone back to the diner. He strolled back across the street to his partner, who'd been serving as witness to Raul and Lupe's argument.

"Raul," she said, her voice softer now. "If the cops get here and we're still fighting, you'll probably be in trouble, so let's just go our separate ways, okay?"

"Don't you care?" he pleaded.

"Yeah, I care," she said. "That's why I'm telling you this. Please go back to the restaurant. I'll just leave, and when the cops get here there won't be anybody to file charges." He was looking at the men on the other side of the street, who were standing there now with their arms across their chests. "I'll talk to them," she said. "I'll explain things. I promise."

"We're still married," he insisted, as if nothing else mattered.

"For just one more year, Raul, so don't blow it for yourself," she said. "And please don't bother me anymore. You're trying my patience. Remember that I can put you right back on the wrong side of the river."

"You wouldn't do that. You'd go to jail yourself for deceiving the law."

They fell silent again.

"What's that?" he asked, nodding at her wrist.

"An ax," she said.

He smiled a little, but he'd already given up. "To cut off men's balls, I suppose."

She chuckled. "Yeah," she said. "If necessary."

They both laughed lightly, a little embarrassed. The two girlish men started pacing on the other side of the street, impatient with the two of them and the police. Then two white women walked casually around them and down to the diner. Lupe pulled her car keys from the shoulder bag. Raul shoved his hands in his pockets.

"I hear you bought a house with Kate—with my money," he said, not meeting her eyes.

She nodded. "It was my money; I earned it."

He looked up, but she refused to make eye contact.

"You should get back to work," she said flatly. "The cops will be here any moment, and I have to go."

"Will you come by, see my mother, or maybe just call sometime?" he asked.

"You never give up, do you?"

"No."

"Well, you should," Lupe said, then walked away. Her sharp strides put her across the street in seconds.

Raul watched as she talked to the two men, their expressions serious, then angry. Lupe's hands moved up and down. After a moment, the men turned and left, obviously disgusted. Raul turned, too, and quietly wandered back to the diner. By the time the squad car arrived, nobody was there.

Forever

alling in love is an obsession driven in part by anger. That's what gives it its urgency. It's an endorphin rush, the kind that helps mothers lift runaway two-ton trucks off their helpless babies. It's why we're here, loving the wrong people over and over and over.

I'm a lesbian activist. Part of my job is to fall in love, over and over and over. Part of my job is to be seen happily communicating, cohabitating, being a woman-loving-woman in the face of danger as well as boredom. Part of my job is to role model, preserving just enough of the threatening stereotypes to remain fashionably on the edge, and yet defying the stereotypes that keep some of us from being invited to our lovers' family homes for the holidays.

I work for a lesbian and gay newspaper, one of those by-the-skin-of-our-asses enterprises that amazes and embarrasses us weekly. I write a political column—political in the sense of elections, not in terms of creating the matriarchy. I make up for it later, not by volunteering at a women's shelter or lobbying for women-only space but by wearing skirts and lipstick and sometimes, in summer, shaved legs. Women aren't so different from any other gender: we like thighs and sighs as much as anyone. I know.

Personally, I like lovers with tempers, women who know that when a junkie is being beaten up by her pimp on the corner of Leland and Magnolia, curled up like a fetus in the middle of the intersection while he repeatedly kicks her, the right thing to do is *not* go to the fire station down the block and tell the uniformed guys relaxing on lawn chairs, but to get out there and hurl ourselves at the prick who would dare do something so vicious.

I like women who can form a fist for something other than a power salute.

I'm thirty-four years old. I come from a good Puerto Rican family which actually stayed together. My father never beat me. I've never been raped. I had an abortion at sixteen that only my mother knows about and a baby boy at seventeen whom I gave up for adoption. I have no money, never have, probably never will. All of this is important.

*   *   *

I'm lying out on a boat with my lover, the early morning sun still rising and glimmering over Lake Michigan. The boat, a tall and elegant sailboat named *Artemis*, is owned by two white women who work in real estate and dream about sailing to Greece. My lover, who's also white, improbably twenty-two, and an art student, resents their innocence. I know this from the look she gives me as she tosses off one-liners that go way over their heads. The sun, still waxing, gives me a headache.

When I go down to the cabin to get some aspirin and refresh my drink—pulpy tomato juice that sticks to my tongue and makes me feel thick—my lover follows. She pushes me flat against the wall so I have to turn my head in order to avoid crushing my nose. She traps me there with her knees pinning the backs of my knees, expertly moving both of her hands under my shirt then down into my shorts, where she presses her thumbs so hard I'm sure she leaves bruises. She moves her left hand down; I'm so wet so quickly she just slides in. Her right hand snakes up under my top, grazing my breasts with her nails, and emerges from my collar. She puts her fingers in my mouth, not delicately but as if she were going to extract a tooth. She makes no sound.

I stand there with my arms outstretched, one holding the empty juice glass, the other the cold can from which I was going to pour a fresh serving. I feel a river running down my legs.

Later, my lover decides to charm our hosts by telling them stories about life in poverty. She talks with a mix of pathos and satire, the ends of her sentences like prickly little daggers. I feel them under my skin and watch our hosts fidgeting in their chairs. I'm never sure what to say at these moments. I know my lover wants support and solidarity; she wants me to side with her—whatever that means—against the easy privilege of sailing on Lake Michigan. She wants our hosts, and me, to feel just a little miserable, but I can't work it up. Instead, I watch them watching her, knowing that they see the chip on her shoulder as well as her luminous white skin and the sharp outline of her clavicles. They look knowingly at each other and laugh, but not at her. They keep enough distance to let her keep her dignity. I'm grateful to all of them. I love her more than ever.

When we get in bed that night, her body is musty and cold. I run my hands on her belly, her shoulders, her long arms. I listen for the rhythm of her breathing. Then her head falls in the space between my chin and chest, her coarse hair lightly scratching my skin. Suddenly, she kisses me with her eyes wide open, almost desperate. And I know immediately: this will not—cannot—last.

※ ※ ※

I go to counseling on Mondays. Sometimes it's an individual session, sometimes it's with my ex-lover, a woman I was with for seven years. She's an actor with a neofuturist group in town, so she's never at a loss for drama or a brand new perspective. We're good lesbians: we've been painfully breaking up for two years. These days I grovel at our joint sessions, having lost all sense of possibilities. Even the therapist turns away, perhaps embarrassed or disgusted, and tells me to please stop.

The worst part of this is that I don't want to go back to my ex-lover. In fact, I don't grovel for love or attention but for explanation. I need to know why things happened, why they had to fall apart the way they did. Before I can go on, I need to understand. I'm getting desperate because I'm fast running out of time: someone, soon, is going to find out about this miserable existence; someone, soon, is going to understand what a lousy role model I really am.

Once, back when we were together, my ex-lover and I hosted my parents for dinner. My father, after too many glasses of wine, passed out on the couch. His snoring was deafening. His cheeks puffed up then shrunk as the noise came blowing out of him. We watched, my then lover, my mother, and me, as our dog licked my father's hand dangling limp off the couch, my father so deadened by the alcohol that he never knew. I thought he was disgusting to have drunk himself into oblivion. But my mother, small and refined, a quiet little bird to his rhinoceros, wouldn't have any of my contempt. "When I think of myself as an old woman, the only person I can picture rocking next to me on the porch is your father," she told us.

My ex-lover and I laughed, in part amused, in part scornful, and in part terrified. We never said so aloud, but we both knew: we never saw ourselves together, wrinkled with age, on a porch or anywhere else.

In retrospect, I realize we were ashamed because we were caught in the trap of believing in the future—in believing we'd last long enough to have one. This hope, as evidenced by everyone I know, is false. Even my mother, who has visions, sees an *imaginary* future on that porch, not a real one. The truth is, she and my father are going to wind up living in my brother's basement, converted into an apartment for their modest use, in a desolated old factory town just south of the city. There won't be a porch or anything to look out at. The reward of staying together so long will be just that, a shared claustrophobia.

Personally, I'd prefer to evolve beyond the concept of lovers, of couples, of love. The future is moot then; the future has no choice but to be now. It strikes me as the most revolutionary lesbian-feminist thing to do. Forget hunger, equality, environmentally correct garbage bags; let's work to eliminate heartbreak instead. Love, coupledom, the right person— they're as anachronistic and elusive as Puerto Rican independence: everybody's for it, but no one's quite sure what it means or how to get it.

I just got a cat. I named it after myself. Now let's see who calls and who answers.

*   *   *

"Miss," the voice whispers to me on the train. I don't bother to look up. It could be anybody, and I'm not in any mood for polite conversation with someone who loved my last column, or for equally polite defenses against someone who hated it. I ignore the voice. Faces peer back from the train windows, reflections superimposed over the shadows rushing by.

I'm in a hurry, on deadline with this week's column in my backpack. This one's a real killer: I happened to have overheard an obnoxious AIDS administrator—who's HIV negative—respond to the shenanigans of a local AIDS activist—who's HIV positive—by saying, "Why doesn't he just die already?" I've got notes. I've got witnesses. Deadlines don't usually mean anything to me (especially if I know my editor's going to lap up my column), but I'm in a hurry today because it's payday at the newspaper. That means it's imperative that I be on time. If I'm not, I won't get my check right away. And if I'm not one of the first to dash to the bank with it, there's always a chance I won't be able to cash it. I can't make the train go any faster, so I watch paper cups, scraps of paper and newsprint fly up, like ghosts, as the train thrashes on, its cargo pungent with summer sweat.

"Miss, miss," the voice says again. It's a man. I continue to ignore him, but this time notice that he has a slight accent. Spanish maybe, or Portuguese.

The train rattles on through the tunnel, tossing the passengers this way then that. The woman sitting next to me on the aisle seat is big and pink. She rolls forward with the train's movement, then to the side. Sweat runs down her temples and chin, disappearing into a roll of flesh on her neck. Her shoulder bumps up against me, but I don't move. She has no clue who I am.

"Miss," the voice says again. The accent's more pronounced now, as is its urgency. I stare up at the man who has suddenly appeared above my reflection in the train window. He's brown-skinned and handsome in an absent-minded sort of way. His nose is straight, almost Roman. I consider that he might be Asian Indian or Pakistani. Maybe an exchange student or a visiting professor needing directions. Then I notice he's holding out a piece of paper.

"This is for you," he says.

I turn my head, my eyes just catching his before they drop to the paper he holds between perfectly manicured fingers. I'm not actually looking at him, but I know that he's nodding, encouraging me to take the paper.

"It is for you," he says again, and this time the paper seems to drop from his hand into mine.

The woman sitting next to me stands to leave and gives her seat to a young white man with a tie and a briefcase.

When I look up again, the Asian man's gone. I hold onto the paper and scan the shifting masses, but I can't find him. The train stops, jostling the passengers. The doors fly open and lines of identically dressed white men with ties and briefcases empty out. The guy next to me stays put, eyes closed. His mouth's slightly agape, but his neck's still straight. I'm tempted to wake him, just to rattle him, but instead I unfold the paper in my lap, half expecting an advertisement for a pizza parlor or escort service.

Typed in a neat serif face, it reads, "I know you know."

* * *

"Oh my god, he ate it," shrieks my twenty-two year old girlfriend as she searches the refrigerator. She leans on the door and laughs. "Can you believe it?" Her red hair stands on end, shocking and brilliant.

"Well, it was a perfectly innocent looking bowl of guacamole," I say. "Why wouldn't he eat it if he was hungry?" I'm sitting at the kitchen table, which is sticky from old spilled coffee.

"Should I tell him? Is there an ethical way to approach this?" she rattles on, amused and nervous. I shrug, peeling off some of the coffee with my neon red fingernail. She lets the refrigerator door close. "What is wrong with you? We just found out my roomie ate a bowl of guacamole seasoned with girl cum, and you're all gloom. Don't you think it's funny?"

She runs her hand through my hair and down the back of my neck. I want her to stop immediately. I want to have no memory—none whatsoever—of last night, of how we started by saying we'd just have a snack in bed, and then, without thinking about it, started offering each other bits and pieces of soft bread with that delicious guacamole, then just our fingers dripping with the stuff. Then there was that moment when she took my hand and pushed it gently down between her legs, and the guacamole smeared against the mauve of her skin, and I was fascinated by the colors and the mix of smells. I needed no encouragement to lower my head. But all I did was look, and feel, and inhale. I never did enter her with my fingers or tongue. I never did make love to her in any recognizable way. Right now I can't think of a single reason why we ever put that guacamole back in the refrigerator.

"I had the weirdest experience on the train today," I say, pulling the note from the Asian man out of my pocket. "This guy just came up and handed me this."

She looks at it. "It's an advertisement for a Meg Christian album, only he's about twenty years too late," she says. She gives me back the note and makes herself busy by clearing the counter of the dirty dishes which have accumulated in the past week.

"He was really deliberate," I tell her. "It wasn't like he was just handing out little pieces of paper to everybody. He came right to me and gave it to me like it was a secret message from a tribal chieftain or something."

She lets the hot water run in the sink, pulls the bowl of leftover guacamole from the refrigerator, and drops it on top of the dishes. Steam rises. "This is the city. Weird things happen all the time," she says. "It's not like there has to be a logical explanation for any of it. Most of the time, you know, there isn't."

I think, Yes, I know. Look at us.

※　※　※

I'm on another deadline—but without a check as reward—when I hear somebody calling my name. I've been taking a lot of heat lately for the column on the obnoxious AIDS administrator, and I really can't deal with one more person telling me I shouldn't be so hard on the guy—he's done so much for the community, and anybody can slip up once—so I try to blend in with the crowd and pretend I don't hear anything. This is particularly hard because, besides the tonnage in my backpack, I'm carrying a twenty-pound bag of special diet cat food that I just bought at the specialty pet store. I'm in the Dearborn-to-State train tunnel at rush hour. All the musicians who normally play here are pressed against the white walls by the commuter crunch. They look flat, wet, and exhausted. Everything smells of sweat. I can't see a thing, can't focus on a single face or outline. There are just too many people. The tunnel's suffocating.

"Hey, *soy yo*," I hear behind me and turn to see Miguel Colorado, a tall, robust-looking painter who lives in my neighborhood. His face is as flat and shiny as pie crust, his nostrils like slits for air. He wraps his fingers around my upper arm and pulls me away from the current. "Are you okay?"

I nod. "Yeah, I'm fine, just a little disoriented. It's too hot."

"You looked pale, like you were going to pass out," he says. His fingers, damp and calloused, are still around my arm. Standing only inches from him, I can smell his body—an acidic, almost bitter odor. I shift my backpack a little then move the cat food from one hip to the other. Finally, he drops his fingers from around my arm.

"Look what I bought," he says, pulling up a yellow plastic bag. From it he yanks a carefully wrapped ceramic hand, its five fingers spread apart against an elaborate backdrop. To either side of each finger, there's a small icon or deity, all garishly painted in primary colors. I recognize it right away as the *siete potencias*, the pantheon of gods revered in *santeria*. But these icons don't look African; instead, they're stereotypically Native American, with feathers and tomahawks.

"That's so ugly!" I say, laughing.

He laughs, too, still holding his prize. "Isn't it, though?" he asks, putting it back in the bag. "I found it at El Talismán, that little place on Lawrence. I wasn't really looking for anything, you know, but I just about fell over when I saw a *siete potencias* with Indians. I mean, *Indians!*"

"What are you going to do with it? I mean, you're not actually going to set it somewhere in your house, are you?" I ask, getting some breathing room as the traffic in the tunnel eases. A couple of people nod at me as they go by, like they know me, but I ignore them. I really can't take anymore feedback on my column.

"Well, I was thinking of bringing it to my Indian support group, but I don't know yet," he says. "I just started going to it, you know, and I don't really know everybody that well yet. I don't want them to think I'm making fun of them or anything. I just thought it was funny."

"Miguel, what are you doing at an Indian support group? You're Mexican," I say, laughing more heartily now.

He shrugs his shoulders, trying to keep it light, but I can see he's serious and even embarrassed now. "Well, I'm both, really," he says. "I mean, I'm too *indio* to be Mexican, and too Spanish to be Indian. I'm fucked, that's what I am. I'm completely fucked up."

I'm trying to muster some sympathy here. I want to put his hand back on my arm, to tell him he's brave for admitting his confusion, for taking this journey. I'm juggling my backpack and the giant bag of diet cat food when I look up and see the Asian man, with his perfect Roman nose, standing across the tunnel and staring at us.

■　■　■

My twenty-two-year-old girlfriend and I are lying on my futon. My cat, who was napping on the bed until we came in, is now perched on the window sill. When my lover and I make love during the day, we usually do it at my house. I'm busy with my column and really can't afford the forty minutes on the train to get to her house. Besides, the incident with the guacamole has really made us nervous about her roommate. He didn't say anything, but it just feels weird, that's all.

There is a problem, however. We haven't talked about it, but it's fairly clear to me that I'm not really interested anymore. It's not that she doesn't turn me on—she does—it's just that I don't want her to touch me. And I don't really want to touch her. So now, instead of having sex in the usual way, we just jerk off together.

Since we're both right-handed, I try to lie on the right side. That way, by putting my arm around her, I can keep her from going any further than I want. I don't care if she kisses my breasts or strokes me. But I'm keenly aware that if our positions were reversed, it'd be very obvious I could do without her. I'm sure *I* wouldn't kiss her breasts or stroke her, and that would probably force us to talk.

Not that she's silent during sex. She's not. She has this remarkable ability to let go, usually in escalating moans. By the time she reaches orgasm, the moans have become full-blown screams. It really is amazing. In all my years of sexual activity, I've never seen anything quite like it.

I admit I envy that release and exhaustion. Although I can come—and come hard, I might add—the experience is often frustrating. My girlfriend, it seems, can reach a crescendo and explode, but me, I just stay there, coming eternally, one time after another, over and over. I realize it sounds enviable, but eventually it just feels suffocating, with my shoulders aching, my fingers splayed and stiff (I sometimes have to use my other hand to unlock them), and this sense that I've been skinned alive.

Recently, as if to bring me out of my coming coma (I know she knows it's not about her), my girlfriend's taken to screaming my name. It startled me at first because she never did that when I used to actually make love to her. My cat, who usually just watches from the window sill when there's sex going on, now comes running, tossing her head, bumping her wet nose against my girlfriend's burning brow.

I've decided whatever's going on is between them.

※　※　※

I am having a problem. In fact, I'm having three problems.

The first is that my editor's incensed because I just lost her an ad account. It seems that the obnoxious AIDS administrator whom I wrote about in last week's column—the one who wanted the street activist dead—is actually part-owner of The Stallion, one of the sleaziest pick-up bars in town and, until now, one of the paper's steadiest ad clients. Neither my editor nor I knew about this when I brought in the column; it would have made no difference to me, but apparently it would have to her.

"Do you realize this man *pays* your salary with his ads?" my editor screams. She's a bulldagger who drives a Lincoln Continental sporting a license plate which reads, "WMN PWR." Right now she's standing over me, waving my check in the air, knowing that as long as it's flapping up there, I'm going to go along with her like a trained seal.

The second problem is that my ex-lover is on the phone, telling me she's reconciled herself to not being able to tell me exactly *why* things happened and that perhaps I should consider accepting this as a resolution to our eternal codependency. She wants to stop going to couple counseling.

"We don't have to know *everything*, do we?" she asks. "You see, I barely remember what happened anymore. You'd have to put me under hypnosis to get the details out of me, and even then I don't know if I could make them make sense."

The third problem is that the twenty-two-year-old is on the other line, asking me if we can have dinner next Monday (which, as she well knows, conflicts with my Monday counseling appointments—a deliberate power play on her part, I assume). She says it's our one-year anniversary. She wants to go to this incredibly expensive Italian restaurant that she, on her puny little art student work-study check, can't afford. I am not dazed by what she expects me to spend—after all, I'm the one with the job and the notoriety—but somehow this thing between us has gotten away from me. How the hell did a year go by already?

"Or maybe," she says. "We should just break up. I mean, relationships never last. I don't know any that do. We're going to break up sooner or later, and the longer we stay in it, the harder it's going to be, the more hurt we're going to be. Maybe we should just call it quits and celebrate the rational side of ourselves. We could toast to a new beginning as friends."

I tell her I have to see her right away.

⁜ ⁜ ⁜

The train is out of control, swinging drastically on the elevated tracks. I'm trying to hold onto the bar above my head, but I'm convinced that every time the car takes a curve, I'm going to throw up. Even though it's the middle of the day, we're squeezed together in this furnace on wheels. There are strangers' faces within inches of my face, strangers' thighs vibrating next to my thighs. I close my eyes, trying to still the rumble in my stomach, until I'm sure I can feel someone's breathing on my breast. But when I open my eyes, there's no one there, just the same sweaty faces all around me. I need some air.

"Excuse me," I say, trying to make my way to the space between the cars. I reach out and grab things, but I don't always know what. I'm drenched, rivulets running down from my armpits. I feel the bodies shifting around me, hesitantly making a way. I can feel their hands passing me around as if I were a dirty postcard at a pervert's party. For a moment it feels reassuring—I know I'm not going to fall with all this soft support—but in an instant I'm embarrassed and disgusted and hope no one's recognized me.

"Jesus fucking Christ, let me out," I say to someone—a conductor maybe, or perhaps a teenager carrying a pale blue beach bag. I don't know. They all look at me blankly. All that happens is that the train takes another manic turn and tosses me against a window, my face smeared against the glass. I hold my jaw because it hurts, but no one, not even the little Eastern European widow standing next to me, says anything.

I manage anyway to get my hands on the door handle, to wiggle it a little so that for one glorious instant I can hear the rush of air and the crazy clattering of metal between the cars. Then the door slams shut again, and I have to pull hard, using my legs against the door frame to pry it open. When I get outside, holding precariously to the link chain running from car to car, it feels like a shrieking wind tunnel. My hair is swept back hard, and I feel sand and dirt hitting my face like tiny needles. All I can think is that I want to hold my heart—that whimpering beast in my chest—but I don't dare let go of the little link chain.

When the train stops, I breathe in and out like a cardiac patient. I can't see because my hair has fallen in front of my face in clumps. But I don't move. My hands are forged around the chain that runs from car to car, and no matter what I tell myself, I can't peel my fingers from it. I can't seem to generate commands from my brain to my limbs.

"Miss, miss," a voice says, and without opening my eyes I

know it's the Asian man standing in front of me between the cars. He is holding another piece of paper out to me.

"What the fuck do you want from me?" I whisper, furious. My hands—which are suddenly barely recognizable as my own—leave the link chain and open, each finger aimed at him like some terrible claw. He's surprised, but he catches my wrists, and we begin to struggle, bouncing each other off the link chain.

"Miss," he says in a panic, but his voice gets lost in the noise. The train starts to pull out of the station, and we're trapped between cars. I see him opening his mouth to say something, but I can't hear him. The train bangs one car against the other, the rails hiss beneath us, and all around the wind is howling.

We wrestle like this until we reach the next stop—the last before the train dives underground to Clark and Division. As soon as we come to a halt at the station, the man, terrified, jumps over the link chain, losing a shoe as he catches the edge of the platform. "You bitch," he shouts, disappearing into the train station. His face is twisted and pained. "I thought you *knew!*" he screams at me, tears running down his cheeks. I'm trying to figure out how he got away from me so quickly and what the hell's going on when I feel the train door behind me pop open.

"Hey, are you okay?" asks a voice. I turn around and see a tall, pink-cheeked public transit policeman. "What happened?" he asks, leading me gently inside the car. "Are you okay? What happened?" he asks over and over.

I sit down and without explanation immediately start crying. The transit cop sits next to me, his meaty arm around my shoulders. When I go to wipe my nose with my hand, I realize I'm still holding the Asian man's mysterious white paper.

* * *

In an aquamarine CTA office, fresh off the train, I sit and drink water from a Styrofoam cup. When I try to explain the situation to the transit police officer and the official Chicago cop sent to take my report, I fully expect them to be assholes, to dismiss me as some self-important dyke radical with a wacko sense of the world. As I look at the three officials in front of me—the transit cop, the real cop, and a woman I think is some kind of sex assault counselor—I'm ready to tell them to go fuck themselves. All I can think of, though, is the twenty-two-year-old, waiting for me outside my apartment. I can't even call her.

"You say you'd seen him around," says the woman. "Does that mean you knew him?"

"Who?" I ask, still thinking about my girlfriend, surely pacing outside my building, wondering what happened, worried and maybe scared. I just want to comfort her, that's all.

"The man who assaulted you," the woman says.

"Him?" I say, remembering the note in my hand. "No, I don't know him. But I see him all the time. He keeps giving me notes." I hand the white paper, still folded, to her. The official Chicago police officer takes it from her and unfolds it very carefully, as if he were defusing a bomb. The beefy transit cop looks over his shoulder, awed. Then the three of them read the note together, their eyes darting from left to right.

"You're María de los Angeles?" asks the transit cop, his face all aglow. "From *OutNews?*"

I nod, but I'm holding my breath, ready to cut this motherfucker down to size if I have to.

He grins, the grin pushing his fat cheeks up so that they almost make his eyes close. "God, I'm so glad to meet you," he says, offering me his hand. "I read your column all the time."

"Apparently, so does your friend," says the woman, handing the note back to me.

I take it cautiously, amazed that they really seem to know

who I am. Then I glance quickly at the white paper, the writing small and carefully crafted, and hold it up to read it.

"Dear María, I read your column every week because I know you know what's it like to be gay and a minority. Very few people understand that when we, who are gay and a minority, enter the gay community we are really exchanging one series of expectations for another, one set of stereotypes for another. The worst part is that the gay community doesn't really accept us if we're a minority, but because we want so much to prove to everybody that we made the right decision, we don't always tell the truth. I'm glad you're not like that. Thanks for representing us so well. Your faithful reader, Rajeesh."

I am suddenly overwhelmed by a hollow feeling in my stomach, as if I'm going to throw up or stop breathing.

※　※　※

"Camila, I need to ask you a favor," I say. I'm standing on the L platform, waiting for a Howard train and talking on a public phone to my ex-girlfriend. I have an unspoiled view of the back porches of a half dozen townhouses, all spilling over with piles of newspapers for recycling, Weber grills, and potted plants. Everything looks cozy, settled. There's not another soul at this train station.

"Listen, María, I want to talk to you, but I have rehearsals in twenty minutes," Camila says. "Can we continue this later? I mean, before Monday, because I wasn't kidding, I really want to stop couple counseling."

I tell her everything in an instant: that I couldn't care less about couple counseling at this point, that Sally's waiting for me in front of my building, our whole relationship up in the air, that I'm running really late because I was nearly assaulted on the train, and that I can't find Sally anywhere.

"I just tried her house," I say. "I was hoping she was still hanging around—although I can't imagine it because it's been forty minutes—and I'm kind of freaked out, and I was wondering—I mean, Camila, you're only a block from my apartment—if you could—please!—just go down there and see if she's still there and tell her I'm on my way, really, and explain what happened."

Camila, to whom I've been confiding all of my ambivalence about Sally, sighs. "I thought you weren't that interested in her anymore," she says. "It sounds like if she's mad and wants to break it off, you're getting what you've wanted all along."

"Look, that's not what I want," I say, suddenly adamant. In the distance I see the blinking lights of a train headed toward the station. The rest of its body is blurry, a mirage in this terrible heat.

My ex-girlfriend laughs. "María, that's *exactly* what you've been saying you want!"

"Camila, *please!*"

She's enjoying this more than she should, but I'm at her mercy, so I let it all go. I tell her the train's nearing, and soon I'll be headed home where, with her help, I'll hopefully find Sally, all arms and legs like a tangle of Pick-up Sticks, sitting on my step pouting and angry but, yes, forgiving—forgiving of me.

"Sally passed the porch test?" Camila asks, teasing.

I stop and try to form the picture—Sally and me rocking on a rustic old porch in some fantasy future—but all I can see is an image of Sally on the train, wearing an engineer's cap and waving at me through a mist. I'm waving back, but I'm choked up and scared. Is the train going to stop? Is she going to jump off? Am I supposed to hop on? And what if I miss?

"Sally passed the test, didn't she?" Camila asks again, but she's not laughing now. There's something almost tender about her tone, something that tells me she's going to find

Sally no matter where she is, and tell her where I've been and why, and all that she knows to be true about how I feel.

"Listen, Camila, I love you," I tell her as the train pulls up. It's one of the newer ones, with less of a rattle and more of a hiss, but I can't hear anything at all. I hang up the phone and climb into an empty car, where it's cool with air conditioning, and the metal on the bars offer my reflection back to me, long and carnival-like.

I throw myself in a seat, lean my head back, and close my eyes. I try and I try, but I can't picture Sally much older than twenty-two, not even at thirty-four, and I think, there is no right person, we will all love the wrong people, over and over and over. Then, as the train yanks itself around a corner, I suddenly see us—me all gray, her with her red hair white-streaked, her arms sinewy under rice paper skin, straddling my rocker with her long legs, telling me I'm not going anywhere.

We Came All the Way From Cuba So You Could Dress Like This?

for Nena

I'm wearing a green sweater. It's made of some synthetic material, and it's mine. I've been wearing it for two days straight and have no plans to take it off right now.

I'm ten years old. I just got off the boat—or rather, the ship. The actual boat didn't make it: We got picked up halfway from Havana to Miami by a gigantic oil freighter to which they then tied our boat. That's how our boat got smashed to smithereens, its wooden planks breaking off like toothpicks against the ship's big metal hull. Everybody talks about American ingenuity, so I'm not sure why somebody didn't anticipate that would happen. But they didn't. So the boat that brought me and my parents most of the way from Cuba is now just part of the debris that'll wash up on tourist beaches all over the Caribbean.

As I speak, my parents are being interrogated by an official from the office of Immigration and Naturalization Services. It's all a formality because this is 1963, and no Cuban claiming political asylum actually gets turned away. We're evidence that the revolution has failed the middle class and that communism is bad. My parents—my father's an accountant and my mother's a social worker—are living, breathing examples of the suffering Cubans have endured under the tyranny of Fidel Castro.

The immigration officer, a fat Hungarian lady with sparkly hazel eyes and a perpetual smile, asks my parents why they came over, and my father, whose face is bright red from spending two days floating in a little boat on the Atlantic Ocean while secretly terrified, points to me—I'm sitting on a couch across the room, more bored than exhausted—and says, We came for her, so she could have a future.

The immigration officer speaks a halting Spanish, and with it she tells my parents about fleeing the Communists in Hungary. She says they took everything from her family, including a large country estate, with forty-four acres and two lakes, that's now being used as a vocational training center. Can you imagine that, she says. There's an official presidential portrait of John F. Kennedy behind her, which will need to be replaced in a week or so.

I fold my arms in front of my chest and across the green sweater. Tonight the U.S. government will put us up in a noisy transient hotel. We'll be allowed to stay there at tax-payer expense for a couple of days until my godfather—who lives with his mistress somewhere in Miami—comes to get us.

※　※　※

Leaning against the wall at the processing center, I notice a volunteer for Catholic Charities who approaches me with gifts: oatmeal cookies, a plastic doll with blond hair and a blue dress, and a rosary made of white plastic beads. She smiles and talks to me in incomprehensible English, speaking unnaturally loud.

My mother, who's watching while sitting nervously next to my father as we're being processed, will later tell me she remembers this moment as something poignant and good.

All I hold onto is the feel of the doll—cool and hard—and the fact that the Catholic volunteer is trying to get me to exchange my green sweater for a little gray flannel gym jacket with a hood and an American flag logo. I wrap myself up tighter in the sweater, which at this point still smells of salt and Cuban dirt and my grandmother's house, and the Catholic volunteer just squeezes my shoulder and leaves, thinking, I'm sure, that I've been traumatized by the trip across the choppy waters. My mother smiles weakly at me from across the room.

I'm still clutching the doll, a thing I'll never play with but which I'll carry with me all my life, from apartment to apartment, one move after the other. Eventually, her little blond nylon hairs will fall off and, thirty years later, after I'm diagnosed with cancer, she'll sit atop my dresser, scarred and bald like a chemo patient.

*　*　*

Is life destiny or determination?

For all the blond boyfriends I will have, there will be only two yellow-haired lovers. One doesn't really count—a boy in a military academy who subscribes to Republican politics like my parents, and who will try, relatively unsuccessfully, to penetrate me on a south Florida beach. I will squirm away from underneath him, not because his penis hurts me but because the stubble on his face burns my cheek.

The other will be Martha, perceived by the whole lesbian community as a gold digger, but who will love me in spite of my poverty. She'll come to my one-room studio on Saturday mornings when her rich lover is still asleep and rip tee-shirts off my shoulders, brutally and honestly.

One Saturday we'll forget to set the alarm to get her back home in time, and Martha will have to dress in a hurry, the smoky smell of my sex all over her face and her own underwear tangled up in her pants leg. When she gets home, her rich lover will notice the weird bulge at her calf and throw her out, forcing Martha to acknowledge that without a primary relationship for contrast, we can't go on.

It's too dangerous, she'll say, tossing her blond hair away from her face.

Years later, I'll visit Martha, now living seaside in Provincetown with her new lover, a Kennedy cousin still in the closet who has a love of dogs, and freckles sprinkled all over her cheeks.

※　※　※

At the processing center, the Catholic volunteer has found a young Colombian woman to talk to me. I don't know her name, but she's pretty and brown, and she speaks Spanish. She tells me she's not Catholic but that she'd like to offer me Christian comfort anyway. She smells of violet water.

She pulls a Bible from her big purse and asks me, Do you know this, and I say, I'm Catholic, and she says that, well, she was once Catholic, too, but then she was saved and became something else. She says everything will change for me in the United States, as it did for her.

Then she tells me about coming here with her father and how he got sick and died, and she was forced to do all sorts of work, including what she calls sinful work, and how the sinful work taught her so much about life, and then how she got saved. She says there's still a problem, an impulse, which she has to suppress by reading the Bible. She looks at me as if I know what she's talking about.

Across the room, my parents are still talking to the fat Hungarian lady, my father's head bent over the table as he fills out form after form.

Then the Catholic volunteer comes back and asks the Colombian girl something in English, and the girl reaches across me, pats my lap, and starts reading from her Spanish-language Bible: Your breasts are like two fawns, twins of a gazelle that feed upon the lilies. Until the day breathes and the shadows flee, I will hie me to the mountain of myrrh and the hill of frankincense. You are all fair, my love; there is no flaw in you.

* * *

Here's what my father dreams I will be in the United States of America: A lawyer, then a judge, in a system of law that is both serious and just. Not that he actually believes in democracy—in fact, he's openly suspicious of the popular will—but he longs for the power and prestige such a career would bring, and which he can't achieve on his own now that we're here, so he projects it all on me. He sees me in courtrooms and lecture halls, at libraries and in elegant restaurants, the object of envy and awe.

My father does not envision me in domestic scenes. He does not imagine me as a wife or mother because to do so would be to imagine someone else closer to me than he is, and he cannot endure that. He will never regret not being a grandfather; it was never part of his plan.

Here's what my mother dreams I will be in the United States of America: The owner of many appliances and a rolling green lawn; mother of two mischievous children; the wife of a boyishly handsome North American man who drinks Pepsi for breakfast; a career woman with a well-paying position in local broadcasting.

My mother pictures me reading the news on TV at four and home at the dinner table by six. She does not propose that I will actually do the cooking, but rather that I'll oversee the undocumented Haitian woman my husband and I have hired for that purpose. She sees me as fulfilled, as she imagines she is.

All I ever think about are kisses, not the deep throaty kind but quick pecks all along my belly just before my lover and I dissolve into warm blankets and tangled sheets in a bed under an open window. I have no view of this scene from a distance, so I don't know if the window frames tall pine trees or tropical bushes permeated with skittering gray lizards.

* * *

It's hot and stuffy in the processing center, where I'm sitting under a light that buzzes and clicks. Everything smells of nicotine. I wipe the shine off my face with the sleeve of my sweater. Eventually, I take off the sweater and fold it over my arm.

My father, smoking cigarette after cigarette, mutters about communism and how the Dominican Republic is next and then, possibly, someplace in Central America.

My mother has disappeared to another floor in the building, where the Catholic volunteer insists that she look through boxes filled with clothes donated by generous North Americans. Later, my mother will tell us how the Catholic volunteer pointed to the little gray flannel gym jacket with the hood and the American flag logo, how she plucked a bow tie from a box, then a black synthetic teddy from another and laughed, embarrassed.

My mother will admit she was uncomfortable with the idea of sifting through the boxes, sinking arm-deep into other people's sweat and excretions, but not that she was afraid of offending the Catholic volunteer and that she held her breath, smiled, and fished out a shirt for my father and a light blue cotton dress for me, which we'll never wear.

* * *

My parents escaped from Cuba because they did not want me to grow up in a communist state. They are anti-communists, especially my father.

It's because of this that when Martin Luther King, Jr., dies in 1968 and North American cities go up in flames, my father will gloat. King was a Communist, he will say; he studied in Moscow, everybody knows that.

I'll roll my eyes and say nothing. My mother will ask him to please finish his *café con leche* and wipe the milk moustache from the top of his lip.

Later, the morning after Bobby Kennedy's brains are shot all over a California hotel kitchen, my father will greet the news of his death by walking into our kitchen wearing a "Nixon's the One" button.

There's no stopping him now, my father will say; I know, because I was involved with the counterrevolution, and I know he's the one who's going to save us, he's the one who came up with the Bay of Pigs—which would have worked, all the experts agree, if he'd been elected instead of Kennedy, that coward.

My mother will vote for Richard Nixon in 1968, but in spite of his loud support my father will sit out the election, convinced there's no need to become a citizen of the United States (the usual prerequisite for voting) because Nixon will get us back to Cuba in no time, where my father's dormant citizenship will spring to life.

Later that summer, my father, who has resisted getting a television set (too cumbersome to be moved when we go back to Cuba, he will tell us), suddenly buys a huge Zenith color model to watch the Olympics broadcast from Mexico City.

I will sit on the floor, close enough to distinguish the different colored dots, while my father sits a few feet away in a LA-Z-BOY chair and roots for the Cuban boxers, especially Teófilo Stevenson. Every time Stevenson wins one—whether against North Americans or East Germans or whomever—my father will jump up and shout.

Later, when the Cuban flag waves at us during the medal

ceremony, and the Cuban national anthem comes through the TV's tinny speakers, my father will stand up in Miami and cover his heart with his palm just like Fidel, watching on his own TV in Havana.

When I get older, I'll tell my father a rumor I heard that Stevenson, for all his heroics, practiced his best boxing moves on his wife, and my father will look at me like I'm crazy and say, Yeah, well, he's a Communist, what did you expect, huh?

■ ■ ■

In the processing center, my father is visited by a Cuban man with a large camera bag and a steno notebook into which he's constantly scribbling. The man has green Coke-bottle glasses and chews on a pungent Cuban cigar as he nods at everything my father says.

My mother, holding a brown paper bag filled with our new (used) clothes, sits next to me on the couch under the buzzing and clicking lights. She asks me about the Colombian girl, and I tell her she read me parts of the Bible, which makes my mother shudder.

The man with the Coke-bottle glasses and cigar tells my father he's from Santiago de Cuba in Oriente province, near Fidel's hometown, where he claims nobody ever supported the revolution because they knew the real Fidel. Then he tells my father he knew his father, which makes my father very nervous.

The whole northern coast of Havana harbor is mined, my father says to the Cuban man as if to distract him. There are *milicianos* all over the beaches, he goes on; it was a miracle we got out, but we had to do it—for her, and he points my way again.

Then the man with the Coke-bottle glasses and cigar jumps up and pulls a giant camera out of his bag, covering my mother and me with a sudden explosion of light.

* * *

In 1971, I'll come home for Thanksgiving from Indiana University where I have a scholarship to study optometry. It'll be the first time in months I'll be without an antiwar demonstration to go to, a consciousness-raising group to attend, or a Gay Liberation meeting to lead.

Alaba'o, I almost didn't recognize you, my mother will say, pulling on the fringes of my suede jacket, promising to mend the holes in my floor-sweeping bell-bottom jeans. My green sweater will be somewhere in the closet of my bedroom in their house.

We left Cuba so you could dress like this? my father will ask over my mother's shoulder.

And for the first and only time in my life, I'll say, Look, you didn't come for me, you came for you; you came because all your rich clients were leaving, and you were going to wind up a cashier in your father's hardware store if you didn't leave, okay?

My father, who works in a bank now, will gasp—*¿Qué qué?*—and step back a bit. And my mother will say, Please, don't talk to your father like that.

And I'll say, It's a free country, I can do anything I want, remember? Christ, he only left because Fidel beat him in that stupid swimming race when they were little.

And then my father will reach over my mother's thin shoulders, grab me by the red bandanna around my neck, and throw me to the floor, where he'll kick me over and over until all I remember is my mother's voice pleading, Please stop, please, please, please stop.

* * *

We leave the processing center with the fat Hungarian lady, who drives a large Ford station wagon. My father sits in the front with her, and my mother and I sit in the back, although there is plenty of room for both of us in the front as well. The fat Hungarian lady is taking us to our hotel, where our room will have a kitchenette and a view of an alley from which a tall black transvestite plies her night trade.

Eventually, I'm drawn by the lights of the city, not just the neon streaming by the car windows but also the white globes on the street lamps, and I scamper to the back where I can watch the lights by myself. I close my eyes tight, then open them, loving the tracers and star bursts on my private screen.

Up in front, the fat Hungarian lady and my father are discussing the United States' many betrayals, first of Eastern Europe after World War II, then of Cuba after the Bay of Pigs invasion.

My mother, whom I believe is as beautiful as any of the palm trees fluttering on the median strip as we drive by, leans her head against the car window, tired and bereft. She comes to when the fat Hungarian lady, in a fit of giggles, breaks from the road and into the parking lot of a supermarket so shrouded in light that I'm sure it's a flying saucer docked here in Miami.

We did this when we first came to America, the fat Hungarian lady says, leading us up to the supermarket. And it's something only people like us can appreciate.

My father bobs his head up and down and my mother follows, her feet scraping the ground as she drags me by the hand.

We walk through the front door and then a turnstile, and suddenly we are in the land of plenty—row upon row of cereal boxes, TV dinners, massive displays of fresh pineapple, crate after crate of oranges, shelves of insect repellent, and every kind of broom. The dairy section is jammed with cheese and chocolate milk.

There's a butcher shop in the back, and my father says, Oh my god, look, and points to a slab of bloody red ribs thick with meat. My god my god my god, he says, as if he's never seen such a thing, or as if we're on the verge of starvation.

Calm down, please, my mother says, but he's not listening, choking back tears and hanging off the fat Hungarian lady who's now walking him past the sausages and hot dogs, packaged bologna and chipped beef.

All around us people stare, but then my father says, We just arrived from Cuba, and there's so much here!

The fat Hungarian lady pats his shoulder and says to the gathering crowd, Yes, he came on a little boat with his whole family; look at his beautiful daughter who will now grow up well-fed and free.

I push up against my mother, who feels as smooth and thin as a palm leaf on Good Friday. My father beams at me, tears in his eyes. All the while, complete strangers congratulate him on his wisdom and courage, give him hugs and money, and welcome him to the United States.

* * *

There are things that can't be told.

Things like when we couldn't find an apartment, everyone's saying it was because landlords in Miami didn't rent to families with kids, but knowing, always, that it was more than that.

Things like my doing very poorly on an IQ test because I didn't speak English, and getting tossed into a special education track, where it took until high school before somebody realized I didn't belong there.

Things like a North American hairdresser's telling my mother she didn't do her kind of hair.

Like my father, finally realizing he wasn't going to go back to Cuba anytime soon, trying to hang himself with the light cord in the bathroom while my mother cleaned rooms at a nearby luxury hotel, but falling instead and breaking his arm.

Like accepting welfare checks, because there really was no other way.

Like knowing that giving money to exile groups often meant helping somebody buy a private yacht for Caribbean vacations, not for invading Cuba, but also knowing that refusing to donate only invited questions about our own patriotism.

And knowing that Nixon really wasn't the one, and wasn't doing anything, and wouldn't have done anything, even if he'd finished his second term, no matter what a good job the Cuban burglars might have done at the Watergate Hotel.

* * *

What if we'd stayed? What if we'd never left Cuba? What if we were there when the last of the counterrevolution was beaten, or when Mariel harbor leaked thousands of Cubans out of the island, or when the Pan-American Games came? What if we'd never left?

All my life, my father will say I would have been a young Communist, falling prey to the revolution's propaganda. According to him, I would have believed ice cream treats came from Fidel, that those hairless Russians were our friends, and that my duty as a revolutionary was to turn him in for his counterrevolutionary activities—which he will swear he'd never have given up if we'd stayed in Cuba.

My mother will shake her head but won't contradict him. She'll say the revolution uses people, and that I, too, would probably have been used, then betrayed, and that we'll never know, but maybe I would have wound up in jail whether I ever believed in the revolution or not, because I would have talked back to the wrong person, me and my big mouth.

I wonder, if we'd stayed then who, if anyone—if not Martha and the boy from the military academy—would have been my blond lovers, or any kind of lovers at all.

※　※　※

And what if we'd stayed, and there had been no revolution?

My parents will never say, as if somehow they know that their lives were meant to exist only in opposition.

I try to imagine who I would have been if Fidel had never come into Havana sitting triumphantly on top of that tank, but I can't. I can only think of variations of who I am, not who I might have been.

In college one day, I'll tell my mother on the phone that I want to go back to Cuba to see, to consider all these questions, and she'll pause, then say, What for? There's nothing there for you, we'll tell you whatever you need to know, don't you trust us?

Over my dead body, my father will say, listening in on the other line.

Years later, when I fly to Washington, D.C., and take a cab straight to the Cuban Interests Section to apply for a visa, a golden-skinned man with the dulled eyes of a bureaucrat will tell me that because I came to the U.S. too young to make the decision to leave for myself—that it was in fact my parents who made it for me—the Cuban government does not recognize my U.S. citizenship.

You need to renew your Cuban passport, he will say. Perhaps your parents have it, or a copy of your birth certificate, or maybe you have a relative or friend who could go through the records in Cuba for you.

I'll remember the passport among my mother's priceless

papers, handwritten in blue ink, even the official parts. But when I ask my parents for it, my mother will say nothing, and my father will say, It's not here anymore, but in a bank box, where you'll never see it. Do you think I would let you betray us like that?

■　■　■

The boy from the military academy will say oh baby baby as he grinds his hips into me. And Martha and all the girls before and after her here in the United States will say ooohhh ooooohhhhh ooooooooohhhhhhhh as my fingers explore inside them.

But the first time I make love with a Cuban, a politically controversial exile writer of some repute, she will say, *Aaaaaayyyyyyyaaaaaaayyyyyaaaaay* and lift me by my hair from between her legs, strings of saliva like sea foam between my mouth and her shiny curls. Then she'll drop me onto her mouth where our tongues will poke each other like wily porpoises.

In one swift movement, she'll flip me on my back, pillows falling every which way from the bed, and kiss every part of me, between my breasts and under my arms, and she'll suck my fingertips, and the inside of my elbows. And when she rests her head on my belly, her ear listening not to my heartbeat but to the fluttering of palm trees, she'll sit up, place one hand on my throat, the other on my sex, and kiss me there, under my rib cage, around my navel, where I am softest and palest.

The next morning, listening to her breathing in my arms, I will wonder how this could have happened, and if it would have happened at all if we'd stayed in Cuba. And if so, if it would have been furtive or free, with or without the revolution. And how—knowing now how cataclysmic life really is— I might hold on to her for a little while longer.

* * *

When my father dies of a heart attack in 1990 (it will happen while he's driving, yelling at somebody, and the car will just sail over to the sidewalk and stop dead at the curb, where he'll fall to the seat and his arms will somehow fold over his chest, his hands set in prayer), I will come home to Florida from Chicago, where I'll be working as a photographer for the *Tribune*. I won't be taking pictures of murder scenes or politicians then but rather rock stars and local performance artists.

I'll be living in Uptown, in a huge house with a dry darkroom in one of the bedrooms, now converted and sealed black, where I cut up negatives and create photomontages that are exhibited at the Whitney Biennial and hailed by the critics as filled with yearning and hope.

When my father dies, I will feel sadness and a wish that certain things had been said, but I will not want more time with him. I will worry about my mother, just like all the relatives who predict she will die of heartbreak within months (she has diabetes and her vision is failing). But she will instead outlive both him and me.

I'll get to Miami Beach, where they've lived in a little coach house off Collins Avenue since their retirement, and find cousins and aunts helping my mother go through insurance papers and bank records, my father's will, his photographs and mementos: his university degree, a faded list of things to take back to Cuba (including Christmas lights), a jaundiced clipping from *Diario de las Américas* about our arrival which quotes my father as saying that Havana harbor is mined, and a photo of my mother and me, wide-eyed and thin, sitting on the couch in the processing center.

My father's funeral will be simple but well-attended,

closed casket at my request, but with a moment reserved for those who want a last look. My mother will stay in the room while the box is pried open (I'll be in the lobby smoking a cigarette, a habit I despised in my father but which I'll pick up at his funeral) and tell me later she stared at the cross above the casket, never registering my father's talcumed and perfumed body beneath it.

I couldn't leave, it wouldn't have looked right, she'll say. But thank god I'm going blind.

Then a minister who we do not know will come and read from the Bible and my mother will reach around my waist and hold onto me as we listen to him say, When all these things come upon you, the blessing and the curse...and you call them to mind among all the nations where the Lord your God has driven you, and return to the Lord your God, you and your children, and obey his voice...with all your heart and with all your soul; then the Lord your God will return your fortunes, and have compassion upon you, and he will gather you again from all the peoples where the Lord your God has scattered you.

※ ※ ※

There will be a storm during my father's burial, which means it will end quickly. My mother and several relatives will go back to her house, where a TV will blare from the bedroom filled with bored teenage cousins, the women will talk about how to make *picadillo* with low-fat ground turkey instead of the traditional beef and ham, and the men will sit outside in the yard, drinking beer or small cups of Cuban coffee, and talk about my father's love of Cuba, and how unfortunate it is that he died just as Eastern Europe is breaking free, and Fidel is surely about to fall.

Three days later, after taking my mother to the movies

and the mall, church and the local Social Security office, I'll be standing at the front gate with my bags, yelling at the cab driver that I'm coming, when my mother will ask me to wait a minute and run back into the house, emerging minutes later with a box for me that won't fit in any of my bags.

A few things, she'll say, a few things that belong to you that I've been meaning to give you for years and now, well, they're yours.

I'll shake the box, which will emit only a muffled sound, and thank her for whatever it is, hug her and kiss her and tell her I'll call her as soon as I get home. She'll put her chicken bone arms around my neck, kiss the skin there all the way to my shoulders, and get choked up, which will break my heart.

Sleepy and tired in the cab to the airport, I'll lean my head against the window and stare out at the lanky palm trees, their brown and green leaves waving good-bye to me through the still coming drizzle. Everything will be damp, and I'll be hot and stuffy, listening to car horns detonating on every side of me. I'll close my eyes, stare at the blackness, and try to imagine something of yearning and hope, but I'll fall asleep instead, waking only when the driver tells me we've arrived, and that he'll get my bags from the trunk, his hand outstretched for the tip as if it were a condition for the return of my things.

When I get home to Uptown I'll forget all about my mother's box until one day many months later when my memory's fuzzy enough to let me be curious. I'll break it open to find grade school report cards, family pictures of the three of us in Cuba, a love letter to her from my father (in which he talks about wanting to kiss the tender mole by her mouth), Xeroxes of my birth certificate, copies of our requests for political asylum, and my faded blue-ink Cuban passport (expiration date: June 1965), all wrapped up in my old green sweater.

When I call my mother—embarrassed about taking so long to unpack her box, overwhelmed by the treasures within it—her answering machine will pick up and, in a bilingual message, give out her beeper number in case of emergency.

A week after my father's death, my mother will buy a computer with a Braille keyboard and a speaker, start learning how to use it at the community center down the block, and be busy investing in mutual funds at a profit within six months.

※　※　※

But this is all a long way off, of course. Right now, we're in a small hotel room with a kitchenette that U.S. taxpayers have provided for us.

My mother, whose eyes are dark and sunken, sits at a little table eating one of the Royal Castle hamburgers the fat Hungarian lady bought for us. My father munches on another, napkins spread under his hands. Their heads are tilted toward the window which faces an alley. To the far south edge, it offers a view of Biscayne Boulevard and a magically colored thread of night traffic. The air is salty and familiar, the moon brilliant hanging in the sky.

I'm in bed, under sheets that feel heavy with humidity and the smell of cleaning agents. The plastic doll the Catholic volunteer gave me sits on my pillow.

Then my father reaches across the table to my mother and says, We made it, we really made it.

And my mother runs her fingers through his hair and nods, and they both start crying, quietly but heartily, holding and stroking each other as if they are all they have.

And then there's a noise—a screech out in the alley followed by what sounds like a hyena's laughter—and my father leaps up and looks out the window, then starts laughing, too.

Oh my god, come here, look at this, he beckons to my

mother, who jumps up and goes to him, positioning herself right under the crook of his arm. Can you believe that, he says.

Only in America, echoes my mother.

And as I lie here wondering about the spectacle outside the window and the new world that awaits us on this and every night of the rest of our lives, even I know we've already come a long way. What none of us can measure yet is how much of the voyage is already behind us.

About the Author

ACHY OBEJAS is a widely published poet, fiction writer, and journalist. Her poetry has been published in *Conditions*, *Revista Chicano-Riquena*, and *Beloit Poetry Journal*, among others. In 1986, she received an NEA fellowship in poetry. Her stories have been published in magazines such as *Antigonish Review*, *Phoebe*, and *Third Woman*, and in numerous anthologies, including *Discontents* (Amethyst), *West Side Stories* (Chicago Stoop), and *Girlfriend Number One* (Cleis). She writes a weekly column for the *Chicago Tribune* and is a regular contributor to *High Performance*, *Chicago Reader*, and *Windy City Times*, among other publications. In 1989, she received a Peter Lisagor Award for political reporting from Sigma Delta Chi/Society for Professional Journalists, for her coverage of the Chicago mayoral elections.

Books from Cleis Press

Fiction

Another Love
by Erzsébet Galgóczi.
ISBN: 0-939416-52-2 24.95 cloth;
ISBN: 0-939416-51-4 8.95 paper.

Cosmopolis:
Urban Stories by Women
edited by Ines Rieder.
ISBN: 0-939416-36-0 24.95 cloth;
ISBN: 0-939416-37-9 9.95 paper

Dirty Weekend:
A Novel of Revenge
by Helen Zahavi.
ISBN: 0-939416-85-9 10.95 paper.

A Forbidden Passion
by Cristina Peri Rossi.
ISBN: 0-939416-64-0 24.95 cloth;
ISBN: 0-939416-68-9 9.95 paper.

In the Garden of Dead Cars
by Sybil Claiborne.
ISBN: 0-939416-65-4 24.95 cloth;
ISBN: 0-939416-66-2 9.95 paper.

Night Train To Mother
by Ronit Lentin.
ISBN: 0-939416-29-8 24.95 cloth;
ISBN: 0-939416-28-X 9.95 paper.

The One You Call Sister:
New Women's Fiction
edited by Paula Martinac.
ISBN: 0-939416-30-1 24.95 cloth;
ISBN: 0-939416031-X 9.95 paper.

Only Lawyers Dancing
by Jan McKemmish.
ISBN: 0-939416-70-0 24.95 cloth;
ISBN: 0-939416-69-7 9.95 paper.

Unholy Alliances: New
Women's Fiction
edited by Louise Rafkin.
ISBN: 0-939416-14-X 21.95 cloth;
ISBN: 0-939416-15-8 9.95 paper.

The Wall
by Marlen Haushofer.
ISBN: 0-939416-53-0 24.95 cloth;
ISBN: 0-939416-54-9 paper.

We Came All The Way from
Cuba So You Could Dress
Like This?: Stories
by Achy Obejas.
ISBN: 0-939416-92-1 24.95 cloth;
ISBN: 0-939416-93-X 10.95 paper.

Latin America

Beyond the Border: A New Age in Latin American Women's Fiction
edited by Nora Erro-Peralta and Caridad Silva-Núñez.
ISBN: 0-939416-42-5 24.95 cloth;
ISBN: 0-939416-43-3 12.95 paper.

The Little School: Tales of Disappearance and Survival in Argentina
by Alicia Partnoy.
ISBN: 0-939416-08-5 21.95 cloth;
ISBN: 0-939416-07-7 9.95 paper.

Revenge of the Apple
by Alicia Partnoy.
ISBN: 0-939416-62-X 24.95 cloth;
ISBN: 0-939416-63-8 8.95 paper.

You Can't Drown the Fire: Latin American Women Writing in Exile
edited by Alicia Partnoy.
ISBN: 0-939416-16-6 24.95 cloth;
ISBN: 0-939416-17-4 9.95 paper.

Lesbian Studies

Boomer: Railroad Memoirs
by Linda Niemann.
ISBN: 0-939416-55-7 12.95 paper.

The Case of the Good-For-Nothing Girlfriend
by Mabel Maney.
ISBN: 0-939416-90-5 24.95 cloth;
ISBN: 0-939416-91-3 10.95 paper.

The Case of the Not-So-Nice Nurse
by Mabel Maney.
ISBN: 0-939416-75-1 24.95 cloth;
ISBN: 0-939416-76-X 9.95 paper.

Dagger: On Butch Women
edited by Roxxie, Lily Burana, Linnea Due.
ISBN: 0-939416-81-6 29.95 cloth;
ISBN: 0-939416-82-4 14.95 paper.

Daughters of Darkness: Lesbian Vampire Stories
edited by Pam Keesey.
ISBN: 0-939416-77-8 24.95 cloth;
ISBN: 0-939416-78-6 9.95 paper.

Different Daughters: A Book by Mothers of Lesbians
edited by Louise Rafkin.
ISBN: 0-939416-12-3 21.95 cloth;
ISBN: 0-939416-13-1 9.95 paper.

Different Mothers: Sons & Daughters of Lesbians Talk About Their Lives
edited by Louise Rafkin.
ISBN: 0-939416-40-9 24.95 cloth;
ISBN: 0-939416-41-7 9.95 paper.

Girlfriend Number One: Lesbian Life in the '90s
edited by Robin Stevens.
ISBN: 0-939416-79-4 29.95 cloth;
ISBN: 0-939416-8 12.95 paper.

Hothead Paisan: Homicidal Lesbian Terrorist
by Diane DiMassa.
ISBN: 0-939416-73-5 14.95 paper.

A Lesbian Love Advisor
by Celeste West.
ISBN: 0-939416-27-1 24.95 cloth;
ISBN: 0-939416-26-3 9.95 paper.

Long Way Home:
The Odyssey of a Lesbian
Mother and Her Children
by Jeanne Jullion.
ISBN: 0-939416-05-0 8.95 paper.

More Serious Pleasure:
Lesbian Erotic Stories
and Poetry
edited by the Sheba Collective.
ISBN: 0-939416-48-4 24.95 cloth;
ISBN: 0-939416-47-6 9.95 paper.

The Night Audrey's
Vibrator Spoke: A
Stonewall Riots Collection
by Andrea Natalie.
ISBN: 0-939416-64-6 8.95 paper.

Queer and Pleasant Danger:
Writing Out My Life
by Louise Rafkin.
ISBN: 0-939416-60-3 24.95 cloth;
ISBN: 0-939416-61-1 9.95 paper.

Rubyfruit Mountain: A
Stonewall Riots Collection
by Andrea Natalie.
ISBN: 0-939416-74-3 9.95 paper.

Serious Pleasure: Lesbian
Erotic Stories and Poetry
edited by the Sheba Collective.
ISBN: 0-939416-46-8 24.95 cloth;
ISBN: 0-939416-45-X 9.95 paper.

Sexual Politics

Good Sex: Real Stories from
Real People
by Julia Hutton.
ISBN: 0-939416-56-5 24.95 cloth;
ISBN: 0-939416-57-3 12.95 paper.

The Good Vibrations Guide
to Sex: How to Have Safe,
Fun Sex in the '90s
by Cathy Winks and
Anne Semans.
ISBN: 0-939416-83-2 29.95;
ISBN: 0-939416-84-0 14.95 paper.

Madonnarama: Essays on
Sex and Popular Culture
edited by Lisa Frank and Paul
Smith.
ISBN: 0-939416-72-7 24.95 cloth;
ISBN: 0-939416-71-9 9.95 paper.

Public Sex: The Culture
of Radical Sex
by Pat Califia.
ISBN: 0-939416-88-3 29.95 cloth;
ISBN: 0-939416-89-1 12.95 paper.

Sex Work: Writings by
Women in the Sex Industry
edited by Frédérique Delacoste
and Priscilla Alexander.
ISBN: 0-939416-10-7 24.95 cloth;
ISBN: 0-939416-11-5 16.95 paper.

Susie Bright's Sexual Reality:
A Virtual Sex World Reader
by Susie Bright.
ISBN: 0-939416-58-1 24.95 cloth;
ISBN: 0-939416-59-X 9.95 paper.

Susie Sexpert's Lesbian Sex World
by Susie Bright.
ISBN: 0-939416-34-4 24.95 cloth;
ISBN: 0-939416-35-2 9.95 paper.

Reference

Putting Out: The Essential Publishing Resource Guide For Gay and Lesbian Writers
by Edisol W. Dotson.
ISBN: 0-939416-86-7 29.95 cloth;
ISBN: 0-939416-87-5 12.95 paper.

Politics of Health

The Absence of the Dead Is Their Way of Appearing
by Mary Winfrey Trautmann.
ISBN: 0-939416-04-2 8.95 paper.

AIDS: The Women
edited by Ines Rieder
and Patricia Ruppelt.
ISBN: 0-939416-20-4 24.95 cloth;
ISBN: 0-939416-21-2 9.95 paper

Don't: A Woman's Word
by Elly Danica.
ISBN: 0-939416-23-9 21.95 cloth;
ISBN: 0-939416-22-0 8.95 paper

1 in 3: Women with Cancer Confront an Epidemic
edited by Judith Brady.
ISBN: 0-939416-50-6 24.95 cloth;
ISBN: 0-939416-49-2 10.95 paper.

Voices in the Night: Women Speaking About Incest
edited by Toni A.H. McNaron
and Yarrow Morgan.
ISBN: 0-939416-02-6 9.95 paper.

With the Power of Each Breath: A Disabled Women's Anthology
edited by Susan Browne, Debra
Connors and Nanci Stern.
ISBN: 0-939416-09-3 24.95 cloth;
ISBN: 0-939416-06-9 10.95 paper.

Woman-Centered Pregnancy and Birth
by the Federation of Feminist
Women's Health Centers.
ISBN: 0-939416-03-4 11.95 paper.

Autobiography, Biography, Letters

Peggy Deery: An Irish Family at War
by Nell McCafferty.
ISBN: 0-939416-38-7 24.95 cloth;
ISBN: 0-939416-39-5 9.95 paper.

The Shape of Red: Insider/Outsider Reflections
by Ruth Hubbard and
Margaret Randall.
ISBN: 0-939416-19-0 24.95 cloth;
ISBN: 0-939416-18-2 9.95 paper.

Women & Honor: Some Notes on Lying
by Adrienne Rich.
ISBN: 0-939416-44-1 3.95 paper.

Animal Rights

And a Deer's Ear, Eagle's Song and Bear's Grace: Relationships Between Animals and Women
edited by Theresa Corrigan and Stephanie T. Hoppe.
ISBN: 0-939416-38-7 24.95 cloth;
ISBN: 0-939416-39-5 9.95 paper.

With a Fly's Eye, Whale's Wit and Woman's Heart: Relationships Between Animals and Women
edited by Theresa Corrigan and Stephanie T. Hoppe.
ISBN: 0-939416-24-7 24.95 cloth;
ISBN: 0-939416-25-5 9.95 paper.

Since 1980, Cleis Press has published progressive books by women. We welcome your order and will ship your books as quickly as possible. Individual orders must be prepaid (U.S. dollars only). Please add 15% shipping. PA residents add 6% sales tax.
Mail orders: Cleis Press, PO Box 8933, Pittsburgh PA 15221.
MasterCard and Visa orders: include account number, expiration date, and signature. FAX your credit card order: (412) 937-1567. Or, phone us Mon–Fri, 9 am 5 pm EST: (412) 937-1555.